He'd missed

He had no idea what was going on. All he knew was that she lay beneath him and he'd been waiting a damn long time to get her there.

One of her soft, hot hands dipped below the waist of his jeans, scoring the small of his back with her nails. Burning need spiked inside him. She slid the other palm around his waist to his stomach. A second later his jeans were open.

Some part of his brain still worked. Searching for control, he lifted his head, his breathing labored. Her blue eyes stared up into his. Firelight chased across her rose-and-cream features.

"You sure about this?"

"Yes." Slipping one hand out from under his sweatshirt, she skimmed her fingers down his clean-shaven jaw. "I want you."

Dear Reader,

Since I began THE HOT ZONE series, I've gotten
a number of letters asking if I plan to write books for
Dr. Meredith Boren and Detective Robin Daly, friends
of the heroine of book one, *Burning Love*. This is
Meredith's story and the first in the next trilogy of
HOT ZONE books.

It's been eighteen months since Meredith painfully broke
off her engagement to fire investigator Gage Parrish and
a year since she learned of his death. Finally ready to
close the door on her past, Meredith goes to her family's
lake house to dispose of the last of his belongings. And
finds the supposedly dead man on her doorstep.

Gage claims faking his death was the only way to keep
Meredith safe after he was nearly killed for his part in
uncovering an arson ring. He is scheduled to testify at
the upcoming trial for the men he implicated, and the
last thing he wants is to involve Meredith, the woman
he still loves, in the danger hot on his heels. But it may
take both of them to make it to the trial alive. I hope you
enjoy the story.

Best wishes,

Debra Cowan

DEBRA COWAN

The Private Bodyguard

Silhouette®

Romantic
SUSPENSE

SILHOUETTE BOOKS
®

Recycling programs
for this product may
not exist in your area.

ISBN-13: 978-0-373-27663-9

THE PRIVATE BODYGUARD

Books by Debra Cowan

DEBRA COWAN

Like many writers, Debra made up stories in her head as a child. Her B.A. in English was obtained with the intention of following family tradition and becoming a schoolteacher, but after she wrote her first novel, there was no looking back. After years of working another job in addition to writing, she now devotes herself full-time to penning both historical and contemporary romances. An avid history buff, Debra enjoys traveling. She has visited places as diverse as Europe and Honduras, where she and her husband served as part of a medical mission team. Born in the foothills of the Kiamichi Mountains, Debra still lives in her native Oklahoma with her husband and their two beagles, Maggie and Domino.

Debra invites her readers to contact her at P.O. Box 30123, Coffee Creek Station, Edmond, OK 73003-0003, or via e-mail at her Web site, www.debracowan.net.

Many thanks to John Hager, for answering my questions about the courthouse. You were a tremendous help! And to Linda Goodnight, nurse, writer and friend, for all things medical.

Chapter 1

At two o'clock on a cold February morning, Dr. Meredith Boren came face-to-face with a dead man.

Asleep in her family's Oklahoma lake house, she'd been awakened by a noise in the kitchen and gotten out of bed to investigate. She'd crept down the long hallway that led from the master bedroom, edged around the foot of the stairs and frozen between the living room and kitchen.

In the melding shadows of night, a man stood over the sink. Meredith's breath lodged sharply in her throat. Moonlight glanced off lean muscle, flashing a series of impressions. His right shirtsleeve was ripped and hanging down his arm. His left hand pressed against his bare shoulder. Something dark stained his flesh and the edge of the sink. The first aid kit lay open on the counter beside him.

Hazy moonlight filtered through the window, mixed with too many shadows to discern the color of his hair. She had a gun in her bedside table. She couldn't see if he had one or not.

He didn't appear interested in anything except patching himself up. Still, Meredith was calling the police.

She retreated a step, intent on slipping back to her room and dialing 9-1-1. At that moment, the man sagged against the counter as if it was the only thing holding him up. The movement brought his face into profile. Pale silver light skimmed his temple, the long planed line of his jaw, part of a strong neck.

Meredith's heart stopped. He looked like…

No, it couldn't be. This had to be a dream, which made sense considering the reason she'd come to the summerhouse at Broken Bow Lake. The cool tile beneath her feet, the whiff of cinnamon from the living area, the underlying metallic scent of blood drifting from the kitchen all felt real, *smelled* real, but they couldn't be.

Gage Parrish was dead, had been dead for a year. It was a dream. Yes, it had to be. If this was real, the man would've seen her from the corner of his eye and reacted.

Operating on less than four hours' sleep out of the last forty-eight, Meredith rubbed her forehead. "No," she murmured.

In the deep stillness, the quiet word shattered the silence.

The man jerked toward her, his hard gaze zeroing in like a laser. Before she could blink, he roared, "What the hell are you doing here?"

She snapped to full attention just as she did when

jarred out of sleep at the hospital to tend a new arrival in the emergency room. This was real. *He* was real. How?

Something fell from his shoulder to the floor—a stained cloth. He didn't grab for it. "You're not supposed to be here."

"Neither are you!" Numb, she stared at the filmy silhouette of her ex-fiancé. She could barely think. Was she breathing?

With his left hand, the man—Gage—gripped the counter's edge. Even in the dim light, Meredith could see his unsteadiness, the waxy sheen of his face.

It was the blood tracking down his shoulder and arm that got her moving. "You're hurt."

She reached him about the time he crumpled into the cabinet, banging it hard. She grabbed his left arm to steady him.

This wasn't possible. He was dead. Dead!

Her mind was unable to process anything except that he was wounded, bleeding. She draped his uninjured arm around her shoulder and started slowly toward the nearest bed. Her bed.

"Are you hurt anywhere else?"

"No," he said hoarsely. "Gunshot."

Surprise jolted her. He'd been shot. Why? How far from here? And completely apart from the gunshot wound, how was it even possible that he was alive? Meredith's head began to pound. Sweat broke out over her body. What was happening was too unreal, too much. Too raw. She couldn't function if she dealt with that right now. Judging from how heavily Gage leaned on her for support, he wasn't up to it, either.

He faltered, his weight pulling her into the wall with him as he propped himself up there.

His warm breath feathered against her face and an unexpected knot of longing shoved painfully under her ribs. She dismissed the emotion.

He struggled away from the wall. "Okay."

She wondered if he'd be able to make it the rest of the way. They reached her room, painstakingly crossed the silver carpet to her queen-size bed and she eased him down on the edge of the mattress. Reaching over, she flipped on the bedside lamp and stood, paralyzed.

Her mind fought to sort this out, to make sense of it. *Believe it.*

Blood smeared his shoulder, her sheet. He groaned, jerking her out of her stupor. He was hurt. She knew how to deal with that. Unbuttoning his black button-down shirt, she eased it away from his injured shoulder, then stripped it off.

"Meredith."

The deep, grainy voice had her looking straight into his pure blue eyes. Eyes she'd thought to never see again. Meredith started at the realization that there was more than pain there. He looked exhausted and… haunted. Tenderness tugged at her. She tore her gaze from his.

Putting herself on autopilot, she palmed off his shoes then eased his legs onto the mattress and laid him back on the pillow. Leaving his jeans on, she knelt beside the bed and got her first good look at the wound. The bullet had gone through his shoulder, entering close to his clavicle. Where the subclavian vein and artery ran. Concern streaked through her.

"You're…not s'pposed to be here."

His words were slurred. Depending on how much blood he'd lost, he'd be getting dizzy. And thirsty.

"It's winter."

She understood his surprise. The lake house was used only in the spring and summer, for fishing, boating and water-skiing. And with her Thunderbird in the garage, it looked as though no one was here.

"Never would've come." He reached up, his fingers brushing her mouth.

Hit with panic and a sudden streak of fear, she jerked away.

"Baby, I'm sorry."

"Be quiet!" She didn't know if he was aware of what he said. She didn't want to hear the endearment he'd always called her. All she cared about was stopping the bleeding.

"Don't move," she ordered. Pushing to her feet, she hurried to the kitchen and grabbed the first aid kit, snatched some hand towels from the nearest drawer then returned to him.

He was still, unnaturally so, and dread stabbed at her. She felt for his carotid pulse. Weak, but there.

"Thirsty," he croaked, his eyes slitted against the pain.

She hurried into the adjoining bath and filled a small glass with water, then returned to hold up his head and help him drink.

After placing the glass on the bedside table, she examined his wound. He was bleeding out externally, not into the chest. Of the two, that was preferable. No broken collarbone, no collapsed lung. The man was beyond lucky. "How long ago did this happen?"

"An hour." He struggled to get out the words. "Or two."

Using one of the towels, she pressed firmly on the wound, noting the deep penetration, the torn flesh, his shallow breathing. "You need to go to a hospital. McCurtain County's hospital is about thirty or forty minutes away."

"No. No hospitals."

"Gage."

"They'll report it." His raspy voice was firm. "No cops."

"But—"

"A cop shot me." His agitation started his blood flowing heavily again. "No hospital."

"You need to calm down." A *cop* had shot him? What was going on? Blood seeped out from under the towel and Meredith pressed harder against the wound.

"Promise me." His face was colorless, and desperate. He groped for her right forearm with his left hand and squeezed hard. "Promise," he rasped, struggling to sit up.

"Be still." Her voice was sharper than she'd intended. She pushed against his opposite shoulder until he eased back into the mattress. "I promise. Now be quiet and let me do what needs to be done."

He must've been using every bit of his strength because when she finally agreed not to contact anyone, he passed out.

Questions hammered at her. Emotions, too. Anger,

confusion, pain. But there was no time to deal with that right now. She could only deal with Gage and his GSW.

Working quickly, she slowed the bleeding, cleaned the wound with alcohol as best she could then stitched the ragged hole near his collarbone. There was no anesthetic. She prayed he'd be out for a long time.

She was cool, precise, steady. She trimmed the stitches. Applied a pressure bandage. Then sat back on her heels and stared at him, her heart thundering in her chest as if she'd run the two hundred and fifty miles from here to Presley.

She began to shake all over.

His dark blond hair reached the base of his neck, longer than she'd ever seen it. His skin was weathered by the sun, putting lines around his eyes that hadn't been there eighteen months ago when she'd broken things off between them. Six months after that, she'd gotten word he was dead. She'd believed it. They all had. So how could he really be here? Really be alive?

Swept up in a sudden swirl of anger and confusion, she wiped streaks of blood from his neck and lower jaw, the back of her hand lingering on the sandpapery roughness of his skin.

His familiar woodsy scent was faint beneath the antiseptic, but she could smell it. Smell him. The lanky, wounded man in her bed was really Gage and he was alive.

She thought she'd shed her last tear over him, but one fell anyway.

Gage opened his eyes, increasingly aware of the searing pain in his right shoulder and torso, a comfortable bed and a soft feminine fragrance. A familiar apricot scent on the sheets, his pillow. Then he remembered. "Meredith," he murmured.

The bathroom door across the room opened and there she was. She paused, soap-scented steam floating around her. Her hair was freshly dried, wild blond curls loose around her shoulders. Her cream-and-rose skin was free of makeup, her blue eyes crystal-bright and wary. She was so beautiful, it hurt to look at her. His memories didn't do her justice.

He'd missed the hell out of her, but despite the telltale spike in his pulse, seeing her was the worst thing for both of them.

Last night hadn't been a hallucination due to pain and blood loss. She was really here. And looking damn good.

"You're awake." She stepped into the bedroom. Her tall lithe figure gloved in a long-sleeved red T-shirt and faded jeans brought to aching life the memory of every bare inch of her.

A slight flush pinkened her skin from her bath. She preferred those to a shower, he knew. And bubbles to bath beads. Apricot or vanilla to any floral scent. Hell. Gage wished he'd forgotten things like that in the past eighteen months, but he hadn't.

Forcing his gaze away, he glanced at the bandage curving over his shoulder and clavicle. "You patched me up."

She nodded.

He made a lame attempt at humor. "Will I live?"

Her eyes went cool. She looked at him as if she

didn't know him. "Won't that interfere with your being dead?"

Ouch. There were a thousand things he should say, all starting with "I'm sorry." He soaked her in, storing away another image for when he had to leave. "You're really here."

"I think that's my line." Her words were as sharp as her laugh.

She was angry. What did he expect? "No one's ever at this house in the winter. I never would've come if I'd known you would be here."

Hurt flared in her eyes. "You're lucky I was or you would've bled out over my sink."

She thought he meant because he didn't want to see her. There wasn't anything he wanted more, but it was dangerous. He couldn't involve her any more than he already had.

Quietly, he said, "Thanks for saving my life."

She gave a curt nod, eyeing him warily. Gage hated it. And there was nothing he could do about trying to correct it before he left. "What time is it?"

"Almost noon. Are you hungry?"

"I could eat." Once he did, he would have to say goodbye. Again.

"All right, I'll get you something." She folded her arms under her breasts and nailed him with a look. "Then I want to know what's going on."

He could tell her some, not all. Nodding, he pushed himself up on his left elbow.

"You lost a lot of blood," she snapped. "You shouldn't try that yet."

"I'm almost there." It was an effort to rise into a half-sitting position against the headboard. He bit back a moan as agony ripped through his shoulder.

She stood close enough for him to see the light brush of freckles across her nose, but the distance between them yawned like a canyon. Her eyes were remote, blank. He wanted to see her smile, just once.

But the steady gaze she trained on him said that wasn't going to happen. He knew what she wanted. Letting out a shaky breath, he asked, "Where do you want me to start?"

"How about with when you died? I'll get your lunch. We can talk while you eat."

She left and he sagged into the headboard. He had no energy, felt as if he could barely lift his hand. Through a fog, he looked around the room where he and Meredith had stayed during their frequent visits.

His gaze moved left to the closet and the piles of clothes stacked neatly beside its open door. In the back of the closet, he could see what he knew was the tip of his slalom water ski. The pale gray walls were missing a couple of pictures, but he couldn't call them to mind at the moment. He felt outside of himself, as if he were barely holding on to consciousness.

Meredith returned with soup, a ham sandwich and a large glass of water on a tray that she set across his lap. "I imagine you're thirsty, but even if you aren't, you need to drink that."

He nodded. "You're not eating?"

"Not hungry."

She'd cut the sandwich in half and still the effort

required to pick it up surprised him. He hadn't realized how weak he was. It took him a while, but he was able to eat without help. By the time he finished the soup, he felt stronger and sleepy.

Meredith walked to the window beside the bed and glanced over. He thought he saw a glint of tears before she looked away and stared out at the gray day, the private dock and lake less than a hundred yards away.

"Your grandparents and I— We thought…"

"I know," he said softly.

She turned, anger crossing her face before she closed it against him. "Why did you let us think you were dead?"

He couldn't tell her everything. The less she knew, the safer she'd be. Breathing past the pain, he stared.

Despite the shadows in her eyes, she was gorgeous. He'd been a self-absorbed fool to let her go. Her creamy skin was velvet-soft. Her blond curls were pulled back in a neat ponytail that made him want to mess it up.

After what he'd done to her, he'd be lucky if she ever let him get close enough to touch her hair, let alone put his hands on her.

Whatever she saw on his face made her frown. "Gage."

"Sorry. I just can't believe I'm seeing you."

"Ditto," she said drily. "Now talk."

"Yeah." He drew in a deep breath, struggling to focus. "Okay, here it is. After you—after we—our—"

After she'd broken their engagement.

"I know what you're talking about," she said stiffly. "Go on."

She'd thought she hadn't regretted returning his ring.

Until six months later when she'd gotten word he was dead and she kept hearing her last words to him over and over. *You don't need to push me out of your life any longer. I want you out of mine.*

They'd been engaged for nearly two years and she'd never been able to get a wedding date out of him. That, along with being repeatedly put second to his job as a fire investigator, had made his obsession with Operation Smoke Screen the last straw. She understood priorities and no one knew better than a doctor that sometimes work must take precedence. But not every time.

So Meredith had finally called it quits. Her last words to him had filled her with guilt. She thought she had gotten past it and now he was here, stirring it up all over again.

His woodsy, body-warmed scent settled in her lungs and notched up a sense of dread. A steadily growing anger. She didn't see how anything he said could be good.

"There was a series of fires. None of us Oklahoma City fire investigators could get anywhere on the case and neither could an investigator hired by an insurance company." He paused, pulling in a shallow breath, looking pale and wasted.

"The residents of one burned-out section went to the State Attorney General with evidence against the torches. He ordered an investigation, asked me to be part of a task force. We discovered an arson ring, a conspiracy made up of gang leaders, city officials and city employees. It was the easiest money they'd ever made, and the more they got, the more they wanted.

"Our evidence was strong. They were all arrested for

murder, conspiracy to commit arson and fraud, and indicted. The trial is scheduled to start in ten days."

"Okay," she said slowly. After sitting with him through the night, never looking away in case he disappeared, some of the shock had worn off, but now it surged inside her again. She shook her head. "I can't believe this is happening."

"It's pretty wild," he admitted.

"Does the trial have anything to do with you being shot?"

He hesitated. "I was in the wrong place at the wrong time."

"That doesn't explain why you let us believe you were dead."

He wanted to touch her, pull her close, but he'd given up that right when he'd let her walk away. And again when he'd made the choice to let her believe a lie. A lie necessary to save his life, but still a lie. "There were two attempts on my life."

Her only sign of distress was the sudden way she paled. Her gaze skipped over him, thoroughly, dispassionately. Looking for proof of his claims. His wounds weren't visible and he wasn't talking about them.

"After those attempts, the Attorney General involved the marshals. They put all of us in WitSec."

She frowned at the term.

"Witness Security," he explained. "Their witness protection program."

"All the investigators?"

"Yes. We argued against it, but by then the decision was out of our hands." Gage had agreed to it in the end because it was his only option, which made him hate it even more. "The police and the AG's office announced that they believed the gang leaders had succeeded in the attempts on our lives. We were all 'pronounced dead,' different ways. One a hunting accident, one a car wreck, one simply disappeared."

"And you," she said hoarsely, "in a fire."

"Yeah." He hated seeing the ravage of grief in her eyes, the pain, the betrayal, but he'd had no choice then. Just as he had no choice now.

"So shouldn't you still be whoever you are now?" She frowned. "And back wherever it is you live now?"

"Getting shot changed my plans. I knew there were medical supplies here and I thought the house would be empty this time of year. It always has been before."

She studied him for a long moment. "There's more."

There was, but he didn't want to give her one iota of information more than necessary. He was determined to keep her safe.

Under the guise of making sure Gage was ready for trial, the marshal assigned to his case had arrived at the house where he'd been living for the past year. It was there that Gage had overheard the man being threatened into killing Gage. If he had to literally give up his life for Meredith, he would. He never should've pushed her out of it.

He'd been half-dead since leaving her, anyway. *Dumb-ass.* He clamped down on the thoughts. She was a regret he lived with every day and looking back on it didn't change one thing. He had to look forward, *move* forward.

He knew he'd lost a lot of blood. He knew how

crappy he felt, but he also knew the risk of staying. "I need to go."

She eyed him critically. "Think you can?"

"I have to."

"How'd you get here?"

"Drove an SUV I've been fixing up. It's at the side of the house."

"You should stay in bed for another twenty-four hours."

The longer he stayed, the higher the chances of Meredith getting involved and he *wasn't* involving her. "It's best."

"Suit yourself."

He wished he could. Tearing his gaze from hers, he asked, "Where's my shirt?"

"I threw it away. It was ruined."

"My leather jacket?"

"It's on a bar stool in the kitchen, along with your laptop. I'll find you something to wear."

She left and came back with a man's long-sleeved denim shirt. "This is Wyatt's. You can borrow it."

"Thanks." Gage was about the same size as Meredith's younger brother, which was good because the only clothes Gage had left here were shorts, T-shirts and underwear.

"Need help getting it on?"

Yes, he did, but if she touched him, Gage didn't think he would be able to make himself leave. "I can do it."

"All right. Let me know if you change your mind. I really don't think you're strong enough to go anywhere."

He sure as hell didn't want to. "I'll be okay."

After studying him for a moment, she shook her head. "I'll get your jacket and laptop."

Her tennis shoes scuffed softly on the hallway's wooden floor as she walked away. Regret welled up inside him. He wanted to stay here, look at her, *be* with her, but he knew he couldn't. He hated this. It was just as painful as it had been a year ago, letting her believe, along with his grandparents, that he was dead.

He sat up and eased his feet to the floor, gripping the edge of the mattress as the room spun. Long seconds later, the dizziness receded. Biting back a moan, he pulled the right sleeve up his arm.

The next thing he knew, he was on the carpet, his shoulders propped against the side of the bed and Meredith was kneeling in front of him.

"What happened?" he asked groggily.

"You passed out."

"Passed out?" Pain pounded through his shoulder, his skull. He felt himself fading. "You have to help me so I can leave."

"And then what? Drive you wherever you need to go? Babysit you? You can't even get dressed on your own." She leaned over, her sweet-smelling hair tickling his jaw as she fitted her shoulder under his, supporting him to his feet.

Light-headed and wobbly, Gage was aware of the blackness at the edge of his vision. He couldn't feel his legs, had no control over them.

Meredith got him prone on the mattress and pulled the blanket over his bare chest. "Don't try that again until I tell you it's all right."

He was fading, his vision blurring, but as she straightened, he said, "Are you okay with this?"

"Does it matter? You can't even walk the three feet to the bathroom let alone out of this house."

"I just…don't want you to get hurt, Meredith."

The look she turned on him was glacial. "It's a little late for that, don't you think?"

Yes, he did. As he watched her walk away, regret rolled over him. The hurt he'd caused her—*them*—was only one more reason he needed to leave ASAP. He'd avoided going to Presley and had come here solely for the purpose of keeping her out of this hell. Instead, he'd made her a target.

Chapter 2

Hours later, Gage jerked awake to the sound of harsh, labored breathing. The wind lashed brutally against the house, crackled in the trees. He thought he'd been done with the nightmare. Staring into the heavy morning shadows, he could still feel the pain and the flames as if they were real. Burning him, burning Meredith. A swirling fiery mix of present and past.

He scanned the room slowly as he tried to level out his pulse. The sheet and blanket were shoved to the foot of the bed. His jeans hung neatly over the back of a chair in the corner, socks tucked into his black running shoes. Meredith.

Gage had tried to call the state attorney general to update him but couldn't reach the man. Not trusting anyone else in Ken Ivory's office, Gage planned to call again later.

Agony bored deep into his injured shoulder and sweat slicked his face, his chest. Fine tremors worked through his body. As pale gray daylight seeped past the blue bedroom curtain, his pulse hammered sharply in his temple. He lay unmoving, trying to deal with the images the nightmare had driven into his fatigued brain. Regret pumped through him like adrenaline. Always the regret. Over his grandparents, over Meredith. Especially over her.

Exhaling a slow breath, he drew a shaking hand down his damp, whisker-stubbled face. He'd gone almost two months this time without having the dream, but sometime during the night, it had grabbed him by the throat. Had him reliving over and over what he couldn't control or change. The lie all his loved ones believed. That he was dead.

The task force Gage had been assigned to had arrested and indicted six coconspirators in an arson-for-hire ring. Those men had ties to a gang, so death for the investigators working Operation Smoke Screen was only a matter of time.

Months ago, Gage had been shot at and escaped unharmed, but he hadn't been so lucky with the second attempt. Yes, he'd survived a vicious pounding by a baseball bat and a lead pipe, but there were aftereffects. Parts of him still didn't operate fully and probably never would.

In addition to a broken nose, jawbone and two ribs, he'd lost his peripheral vision on the right side. A fracture to his orbital rim had damaged the optic nerve.

After two surgeries, he was amazed he didn't look like a completely different person.

Local law enforcement already had plans in the works to provide protection for all the investigators and witnesses, but after Gage had been beaten and left for dead, and a day later, the ATF agent assigned to the task force had also been attacked, the State Attorney General had requested assistance from the Marshals Service.

Gage's time had come a year ago. He'd been unable to tell the grandparents who'd raised him. And Meredith wouldn't welcome any contact, a fact she'd made emphatically clear six months before when she'd returned his ring. Per instruction from the marshals, he had ignored the phone calls from his best friend and firefighter, Aaron Chapman.

As clearly as if it were happening right then, the images scrawled across his brain in painful technicolor. The bitter February cold sliced at him like a knife, so sharp it stung his lungs. The tang of gasoline and winter-fallow earth mixed with the faint aroma coming from the coffee plant a mile away.

As his life had gone up in flames, Gage thought about his grandparents and how unfair this was to them. Thought about Meredith and wondered if she would even care when she heard the news.

He felt sick to his stomach and slowly became aware once again of where he was. In the present, with his ex. Frustration and helplessness over the situation still ate at him like acid.

He now lived as a mechanic in the northeastern Texas town of Texarkana. He was sick to death of reminding himself that this lying was necessary. That he was doing it for his job, doing it to protect those he loved, to protect future victims.

The past months had been spent with him alternating between self-loathing and flat-out ambivalence. He'd grown impatient and more uncertain that the deliberate erasure of his life made a damned bit of difference.

He had found himself sinking into an apathy he'd never experienced. His job had always motivated him, challenged him, but now it was a ball and chain. He wanted his life back and he was starting to wonder if it would ever happen.

Noises penetrated his thoughts. Down the hall, he heard a drawer opening, water running. He pinpointed the sound as coming from the kitchen. He hadn't had the nightmare in a while and he knew why he'd had it now. Meredith.

Seeing her had sprung the lock on Gage's tightly guarded memories. He'd thought there was no regret left in him, but the disbelief, the dazed shock and apprehension on her face last night had proved him wrong.

His chest still ached from the emotion that exploded inside him upon seeing her. He felt raw, exposed. Unprepared. Why was she at her family's summer lake house in the dead of winter?

A chill settled over him and he shifted uncomfortably against the burning pain in his shoulder. He'd spent the past year consoling himself with the thought that at least his grandparents and his ex-fiancé weren't involved in this mess, that he didn't have to worry about their safety. Finding Meredith here had shot that all to hell. She'd probably saved his life and the longer he stayed, the more he endangered hers.

She'd come here to bury the past; instead it had blown up in her face. Throughout yesterday and last night, Meredith made hourly visits to check Gage for fever, shock or signs of more bleeding. She made him drink plenty of water and gave him antibiotics as well as ibuprofen, which was all she had for pain. In between, she had cried, paced and fought the urge to yell at him.

Gage wasn't dead. He hadn't ever been dead. She'd taken his pulse, touched his flesh and yet she could barely absorb it.

At first, she was numb, then she felt…everything. By late last night, incredulity had given way to nerves. And fear for him. She didn't buy his explanation of being shot because he was in the wrong place at the wrong time, but she hesitated to press for an answer. She wanted to know and yet she didn't.

For the past year, he'd lied to her, to everyone. She understood why, but that didn't stop the feeling of betrayal or resentment. It wasn't surprising that he'd given up his whole life for his job. Everything came second to the fire department and always had. Including her.

After moving his silver SUV into the garage next to her car, she'd dozed off and on in the twin bed across the hall with the door open so she could hear and see him.

Except for her interruptions, he'd slept deeply the past

eighteen hours. He appeared to be still asleep when she rose at dawn and went to the kitchen to start coffee. On the way back to her room, she stopped to check him again.

There was enough watery light to make out his motionless, half-naked body. He'd kicked the quilt and sheet to the foot of the bed. Last night, she hadn't had the time or the presence of mind to notice any physical changes, but she did now. He'd always been rangy, and now he'd become sleeker, more defined. His arms and shoulders were solid slabs of muscle.

The dark lashes laying against his winter-reddened skin were the only soft thing on his sharply planed face. She'd removed his jeans, making him as comfortable as possible and now her gaze skimmed his hard chest, lingered on the lean hips in gray boxers. When she caught herself staring at his plank board–hard abdomen, she mentally shook herself.

Pressing the back of her hand against his cheek, she registered light perspiration, but no clamminess, no fever. She didn't realize she was caressing him until her gaze returned to his face. And found him watching her.

His blue eyes heated in the way that had always sent a shiver through her. And still did, she realized with a jolt as she withdrew her hand.

He gave her a weak grin. "Couldn't wait to get me out of my clothes, huh?"

"How can you joke about this?" she snapped.

He shrugged and she saw it then—the bleak shadow of pain in his eyes. He was only trying to cope with his injury, she chided herself. And maybe some of the same awkwardness she felt.

Off balance and unsure about exactly how to act with him, Meredith decided the best thing for her to do was deal with him as she would any other patient. Professional, efficient, distant enough to remain clinical about his injury.

She eyed his pressure bandage. Without access to a hospital or clinic, she couldn't be sure he *wasn't* bleeding inside so she had left on the thick ABD pad a little longer than twenty-four hours. There was nothing more she could do except keep a close eye on his pulse and blood pressure.

The supplies she'd had on hand were better than she would've gotten from a drugstore first aid kit. Since both she and her brother Wyatt were doctors, they kept the lake house stocked with bandages, sutures, antibiotics and syringes. Through the years, they'd needed those things plenty of times due to fishing or waterskiing accidents.

"What do you think?"

"You can wear a regular bandage now. What you need is food and lots of rest. And you can't exert yourself."

He levered himself up on his good hand.

Startled at his movement, Meredith reached for him. "What are you doing? Did you hear what I just said?"

"I'm sitting up." He winced. Though he didn't push her away, he didn't accept her support, either. He got his feet on the floor and remained on the edge of the bed.

She pressed two fingers to his carotid artery, feeling

for a rapid or thready pulse. It was fast, but not danger-ously so. Not yet, anyway. "You used to be a para-medic. You should know better."

"I'm a little rusty," he said drily. "But I remember."

"So go easy, all right?"

He nodded.

"Are you dizzy at all?" she asked quietly.

"I'm fine."

She studied him. He was pale, but his eyes were lucid. "I'll change your dressing. Be right back."

A few moments later, she returned with fresh sup-plies. His head was bowed, but he straightened when she halted in front of him and placed the items on the night-stand.

"Doing okay?"

"Yeah," he rasped.

She carefully removed the ABD bandage then began to clean the sutured wound with antiseptic.

Hissing in a breath, his body went rigid. Meredith's attention locked on his broad chest, the hair there that grew a little darker than the sandy-blond on his head. As awareness tugged low in her belly, she forced her at-tention back to his shoulder.

He watched as she checked for inflammation, heat, additional swelling.

"Nice stitch job," he said in a slightly rough voice.

"Thanks."

"You still at Presley Medical Center?"

"Yes."

"And still working with the senior citizens pro-gram?"

Her gaze met his, seeing the same memory there that flashed in her own mind. It was how they'd met. His grandmother was part of the city's planning committee for seniors' activities and so were Meredith and her mother. Millie Parrish had known Meredith all of two weeks when she and Meredith's mother, Christine, set up Gage and Meredith on a date.

From their first meeting, there had been something special between them. They'd shaken hands and it was as if a current of energy traveled from her to him. Nothing like that had ever happened to her with any other man.

"Yes, still working with the older people." Shoving away the memory, she reached for a fresh gauze pad.

He grazed a hand against her thigh. "I want to clean up."

Aggravated at the way his touch burned through her jeans, she ignored the sensation and considered his freshly swabbed wound. "Your dressing can't get wet. I'll tape some plastic over it and you can take a bath."

"Great." He dragged a hand down his face.

As she took in the whisker stubble, the exhaustion on his face, she felt battered by the past and by the staggering reality of the present. "I'll see what there is to cover your bandage, then I'll run your water."

He nodded as she left the room. Under the kitchen sink, she found her mom's neat stash of plastic bags from a discount store. Meredith took one and retraced her steps to the bedroom, then walked past Gage into the restroom.

She turned on the tub's faucet and adjusted the water temperature. When she turned, she found him in the doorway. Features strained, he braced himself against the jamb. His boxers dipped low on his hips.

This awareness she had of him irritated her. "When I said don't exert yourself, I meant doing things like walking without support."

"I've got all the speed of a snail. I'm okay." He moved to her left, his good hand gripping the edge of the counter.

Meredith eased past him to get a clean towel, then hung it within easy reach of the tub. Turning back, she caught his dark woodsy scent and a faint hint of clean sweat. He smelled more than good. He smelled familiar, reassuring.

She wanted to bury her face in his neck and breathe him in, pretend the past eighteen months had never happened. But they had and both of them were changed because of it.

When the bath was more than half-full, she turned off the water and stepped aside. His good hand clamped on the edge of the counter and the flex of muscle up his forearm told her he was using a fair amount of strength to hold on.

Her gaze slid down his chest and to the waist of his boxers. Under her regard, the thin bands of muscle across his stomach clenched and his reaction had her looking away.

Okay. She was letting him affect her way too much. After a moment, her brain kicked in. Reaching around him, she scooped up the plastic bag. She double-folded it, then taped it snugly over the bandage so it was covered. "There you go."

She gently smoothed the edges, her hand moving over the hard curve of his shoulder.

Abruptly, he drew back. "I'm good. I'll yell if I need anything."

That heat flashed in his eyes again, making her aware that she'd been practically petting him. She needed to get out of here, although she wouldn't walk away from any other patient at this point. "You're probably going to need help getting in."

"I'll be fine, Meredith."

The steady, unreadable look on his face had her edging past him, careful not to touch as she stepped into the hall. "I won't close the door completely. I'll be right here. Call me if you need help getting in or out or…with anything else."

"Yeah."

She pulled the door toward her, leaving it ajar. "Toss out your underwear and I'll wash them."

"What am I supposed to wear?"

"There should be something around here that will fit." Either of his own or her brother's.

After a moment, he said, "Here."

Looking down, she saw his boxers in the V of the open doorway. Long seconds later, the slosh of water and a groan told her he'd settled into the tub. She picked up his underwear, examining the blood-stiffened waistband.

She leaned back against the wall, listening. Waiting. Reviewing her treatment of his injury. He'd be gone soon and she'd probably never see him again. The thought hurt her heart.

A splash sounded then a heavy thud against the tub.

Before she could ask, he offered, "Dropped the soap."

"Oh." Hit with a sudden image of the two of them in that tub, naked, she exhaled a shaky breath. The memories slipped in. The veins cording his neck, the tapering of his wide shoulders to lean hips, the way his hair clung to the wet sinew and muscle of his chest. She could almost feel his slick warm flesh beneath her hands.

She swallowed hard, grateful when he rasped, "What about Aaron?"

Glad to have her thoughts occupied by Gage's best friend rather than his naked body, Meredith turned her head toward the open doorway. "He's been working some of his off days with the Oklahoma City fire investigator's office. He wanted to work at Presley, but Terra and Collier can't hire anyone else so he decided to go to Oklahoma City."

Terra Spencer, one of Meredith's best friends, and Collier McClain were the two fire investigators allowed by Presley's budget.

"Aaron wants to be a fire cop? He never had any interest in that before."

"That was before you—what happened to you."

"What do you mean?"

She heard the frown in his voice. He and Aaron had grown up together, attended the fire academy and fought blazes in the same station house for years. "He's never quite believed the story we were told."

"Do you think he suspects?" he asked quietly.

"I don't see how." She eased back against the wall.

"Maybe I'm naive, but I sure never would have guessed the truth. In my job, when people die, they really die."

There was a long moment of silence. "Have you talked to my grandparents?"

"I saw them last week. At the cemetery."

He cursed. It was weak, but she heard it and she knew why. It had been the anniversary of his death.

"I helped your grandmother make the funeral arrangements." She paused, working to still the quiver in her voice. "Your grandfather and I scattered your ashes—well, *someone's* ashes—off the dock out back."

Talking about it brought back the heartbreaking pain on Owen's and Millie's faces, the devastation and denial Meredith had felt upon hearing the news of his death.

"Meredith, I had no choice. The situation was out of my control."

She believed him, but she couldn't keep the anger from her voice. "It's a little hard to take in, Gage."

"I know."

The ache beneath his words reminded her that things hadn't gone the way he wanted, either. "I don't want you passing out."

"I'm okay." He sounded drowsy.

She had to keep him talking. "So whose ashes were those?"

"The Marshals Service said it was a body donated to one of the state's medical schools. They had my DNA, dental records, everything they needed to make my death believable."

She was glad Gage was alive. Relieved and grateful, but she wanted to know if it had been as difficult for him to pretend to be dead as it had been for his grandparents to deal with the loss of their only grandchild. For Meredith to deal with the fact that the only man she'd ever loved was gone.

She tried to tamp down her resentment, thought about the man and woman who'd raised Gage after his teenage junkie mother died in a meth house. "Do you want me to tell Owen and Millie anything?"

"You can't," he said quickly. "I won't put them at risk. I never meant to put *you* at risk. Hell, you were the last thing I needed."

Which was why she'd finally walked away. The old wound cracked open and bitterness welled up. "That sounds familiar."

"No, Meredith. That isn't what I meant."

"It's okay." There was hurt on both sides. Hadn't she told him she wanted him out of her life? She'd gotten that, all right. Completely. "How're you doing?"

"Fine."

Was his voice uneven, his strength fading? "You should get out of the tub."

"Yeah."

"Do you need help?"

He gave a hoarse laugh. "That wouldn't be a good idea for either of us."

He was right. Even so, she stood poised to go in at the first hint he needed help. The slosh of water told her he'd managed to stand on his own. "Gage?"

"I'm all right."

He didn't sound all right, but Meredith stayed where she was.

On a groan, he asked, "That swing still on the back porch?"

Her gaze cut to the door. Making conversation was probably his way of dealing with the pain or struggling to stay alert, but why did he have to ask about the swing? They'd all but had sex in it. Talked, laughed. Gotten engaged. It was an effort to keep her voice steady. "Yes, it's still there."

No answer.

"Gage?"

"Just need…a sec." He sounded winded.

"Are you dizzy?"

No answer.

Meredith straightened, concerned. "Gage!"

"M'okay."

The slurred words had her dropping his boxers and pushing open the bathroom door. The toilet lid was closed and he sat there with his good shoulder braced against the wall to his left. His lower half was barely covered by the white towel she'd left.

He'd done too much, too soon. Glad to see the plastic had protected the bandage, she moved in front of him. "I let you stay in there too long."

"Just…wait."

His waxy skin had her pressing a hand to his forehead to find it slightly clammy. She checked his pulse and though rapid, it was strong. "Do you feel faint?"

"No, but not steady, either." He straightened and immediately clutched her hip with his good hand.

Meredith's heart skipped a beat.

"Sorry."

"No problem."

His hold gentled, but he didn't let go. It didn't matter that he touched her strictly for support or that he wasn't even looking at her. Despite her determination not to let him affect her, sensation shot straight to all her nerve endings.

She breathed in his fresh-soap scent, uneasily aware of the weight of his hand on her, the heat of his palm. An ache lodged in her throat and she couldn't stop her gaze from dragging over him. His stomach was taut with muscle and sinew. Powerful thighs, one almost completely exposed by the parted towel, were dusted with hair a shade lighter than his golden skin.

He wasn't pretty-boy handsome, but there was an un-adorned maleness about him that drew the eye. The combination of his solid, planed features and his melt-ingly blue eyes, kind eyes, made for a compelling face. Before she even knew what she was doing, she grazed the tips of her fingers against his temple.

Gage's hand curled into Meredith's flesh. For a long moment, he sat there and let her warmth seep into him, her light apricot scent. He barely had the energy to stand, but he felt a stirring in his body. Pain throbbed in his shoulder and after a few seconds, he was able to focus his mind there, and only there.

"Gage?"

He stared up into her gorgeous blue eyes. "I'm ready."

She looked doubtful, but stepped back so he could stand. Flattening his palm on the wall, he levered himself up. Weakness washed through him and he stilled. He wanted to get back in bed and he wanted Meredith with him. He wanted to stay here with her, but he'd put her in enough danger.

Dipping her knees, she braced her shoulder under his good one and slid a slender arm around his waist.

He draped his arm around her and they started slowly toward the door. "Thanks," he said.

They had taken only two steps when the towel slipped. Despite making a grab for it with the hand on his injured side—which hurt like hell—Gage was too late. The towel fell.

"No way," he gritted out.

Meredith's breath left her in a rush. "Oh."

Damn. She'd seen him bare-assed naked plenty of times and she probably only had her eyes on him this time for less than a second, but Gage felt his body tighten.

Flushing a deep rose, she quickly scooped up the towel, then pulled it around his waist, holding the edges together.

Her reaction was calm, but the feel of her cool fingers against his flesh had Gage anything but. He went hot, muscles clenching. Hell!

She was acting as if nothing had happened and despite his body's reaction, he didn't have the energy to act any differently.

As they shuffled out of the restroom and back to his bed, her hand stayed at his hip, keeping the towel secure. She eased him down onto the edge of the mattress then straightened, still pink-cheeked.

Turning away, she went to the closet and knelt in

front of a neat mound of clothes on the floor then returned with a pair of blue-and-white-striped boxers and black sweats. *His* boxers and her brother's sweats.

Her gaze didn't quite meet his as she handed him the garments. "Do you need help with these?"

"No, I can do it." Maybe. Maybe not. But it was better for both of them if she didn't touch him.

Glancing again at the items in front of the closet, he realized with a sinking feeling what he was seeing. She was getting rid of his stuff. *This* was why Meredith had come to the lake house in the dead of winter.

She was putting him in the past, moving on. He told himself not to ask, but he did. "Are you seeing someone?"

Startled, her gaze swerved to his and for an instant, he saw loss and regret on her face. He thought she wouldn't answer. It was none of his business, but he had to know.

She glanced away. "Not exclusively."

The idea of some other man putting his hands on her had a red mist hazing Gage's vision.

He had no right to want anything from her, not after what he'd done. Over and over, he'd put his job ahead of her, of *them.* She'd tried talking to him about it, pleading with him to step back just a little from work, especially from Operation Smoke Screen, but he couldn't—*wouldn't.*

When she'd broken their engagement, she had said his job had taken over his life. Neither of them could have guessed that it literally would.

Now, he didn't even have the job he'd chosen over her. He had a life that wasn't his own, no family, no nothing.

The past year had brought home to him in brutal terms what a mistake he'd made with Meredith. For six months after she'd walked away, he'd let himself be swallowed up by this case, had refused to admit he was to blame for their split, but since then, he'd had plenty of time to think about it. To admit it.

Her gaze held his, her blue eyes now remote. He wanted to pull her into his lap and kiss her until she went soft for him, but she'd lay him out flat if he tried it.

He might never touch her again, see her again and the thought snarled in his gut like a hook. He couldn't change the hurt he'd caused, but he could do one thing.

She began to untape the plastic over his bandage. Half expecting her to pull away, he took her closest hand.

She stiffened as she stared down at him, but didn't move.

One of the hardest things he'd ever done was look straight at her. "I hate that I hurt you."

Her eyes widened, turned wary. "Gage—"

"Let me." He squeezed her hand. When she remained silent, he continued, "I know it's a cliché, but if I could go back, I'd do things differently. For the rest of my life, I will regret pushing you away."

Her eyes darkened and for a heartbeat, he hoped she might say she forgave him.

Then her face went carefully blank and she slid her hand from his, crumpling the plastic bag she'd removed and turning to go. "Put it in the past. I have."

Chapter 3

Gage followed Meredith's orders to stay in bed. Throughout the day, she moved in and out of his room, keeping a close eye on him. At first, his body reacted every time she walked in. Part of that was due to having her hands on him earlier when she'd held that towel in place, teasing him with the possibility that her touch might slide lower.

Yes, he was a dog, but he couldn't stop thinking about it.

He slept quite a bit, which satisfied Meredith enough to bring him what she probably thought was his laptop. It was Ed Nowlin's laptop. Just the thought of what happened with the marshal had a firestorm of anger flashing through Gage.

He reined in his fury, hoping like hell the computer

would give him some sort of clue about who had coerced the man into trying to kill him.

After sunset a couple of hours ago, he and Meredith had eaten dinner. He'd returned to bed as he'd promised, rebooted the marshal's laptop that he had snatched earlier from the man's car and continued opening files. Looking for something about the murder attempt on him or any of the other witnesses. About why he'd heard Nowlin mention the name Larry James, the disgraced ex-fire investigator Gage suspected of being the mastermind behind the arson plot. He needed something. Anything.

While he worked, Gage could hear Meredith puttering around the house. Which distracted him, slipping images into his mind that he didn't want there. Like the two of them on the back porch in that swing. Kissing, touching, undressing. And the time they'd tried to have sex there. It hadn't worked, but they'd had fun trying.

That memory kicked off others. Her amazingly soft skin against his, the delicate line of her spine beneath his hands, the sweet taste of that place on her nape. Kissing her there always pulled this breathy, pleading sound from her that charged him up like a straight jolt of adrenaline.

Drawn out of his thoughts as she passed by his room, he wondered if any other man knew those things about her. The possibility had anger roaring through him and he tried to stop thinking about her. About *them.* But the memories crept in like smoke, circling him until he was lost in them before he even realized what had happened. Which was why it took him staring at the computer screen twice before he realized what he was seeing.

He'd opened a desktop icon innocuously labeled "shortcuts," which brought up a drawing. The schematic of a building.

There was no address, no specific room delineation or boundaries, but there was a detailed rendering of the ventilation system for the eight-story building. Enough detail to have him cursing under his breath and zooming in on the diagram. A hard knot in his chest told him the drawing was likely that of the Oklahoma County courthouse, where all the witnesses would congregate. Nowlin could've easily obtained the schematic by using the ruse that he was doing prep work for security at the upcoming trial.

All the serial arsons Gage had worked in Operation Smoke Screen had started in the ventilation system. No remains of the accelerant had ever been found at the scenes. Even collecting samples immediately after the fires hadn't yielded anything to test. But Gage knew by the total involvement of the buildings, by the speed of the burns, by the multiple points of origin that there had been an accelerant.

Even ATF Agent Wright hadn't been able to figure out the mystery accelerant. That only strengthened Gage's suspicion that the arsonist was someone with extensive fire knowledge, enough to invent a burn agent that evaporated. Someone like Larry James, who had vowed revenge against the city employees he thought had wrongfully fired him. The city employees who were now awaiting trial for arson, fraud and murder.

Gage had notes back in Texarkana full of chemical

combinations, results of tests he'd performed to no avail. The schematic on the computer screen wasn't much, but it was a starting place. It was too much of a coincidence that the man who'd been coerced into trying to kill Gage would have this kind of detail. Which likely meant that whoever had threatened Nowlin wanted the diagram and was planning something explosive at the courthouse when the trial began.

Gage had already planned to leave Meredith's tomorrow morning. Not because being this close to her was torture, although it was, but because his staying put her in danger. The thought of walking away from her again ripped at his insides.

"Gage?"

The impatience in her voice meant she'd tried to get his attention more than once. He stared up into her blue eyes. "Yeah?"

"Do you want to keep any of these clothes?" She gestured to the stack in front of the closet. "I can bag them up for you."

The fact that she had come here to get rid of his things still annoyed the hell out of him.

"There are a couple more pairs of boxers, several T-shirts and several pairs of shorts."

"All of them, I guess." It was difficult to keep the frustration out of his voice. He had no right to be resentful, but he was. How could she discard his things as if they were nothing more than clutter? As if *he* were?

That wasn't fair to her and he knew it. He was the one who'd done the discarding first. As she turned toward the hall, he said, "I'll be leaving in the morning."

She looked over her shoulder, mouth flattening with disapproval. "Not before I say you're up to it."

He stored away the memory of her sky-blue eyes, her refined features, that tempting mouth. He wanted to stay, but if Nowlin found this place or Meredith, Gage would never forgive himself. "It's for the best. This way, you won't be involved any further."

"You were shot. You lost a lot of blood. If you leave too soon, you'll end up flat on your face."

It didn't matter. If he suffered a setback, it had to be somewhere away from her.

She must've seen the decision on his face. Irritation flashing across her features, she threw up a dismissive hand and started out of the room.

"Meredith." He swallowed around the tightness in his throat. "I don't know how to say goodbye to you."

She froze. After a long pulsing moment, she whispered, "You just did."

She walked out, just as she had eighteen months ago.

"I don't know how to say goodbye to you."

Gage's words had hit her with the same bone-aching loneliness she'd felt when they'd split up.

And it annoyed her, as did his announcement that he was leaving. Being annoyed made no sense because saying goodbye to him was exactly why she'd taken two weeks off work and come down here. It was his physical well-being that concerned her, Meredith told herself. And his stubbornness. It still made her want to wring his neck. He wasn't recovered enough yet to go, but she knew that look in his eye, that forged-steel cast to his jaw. He wasn't changing his mind. The man drove her crazy.

Proven by the fact that she couldn't dismiss the image of him naked this morning. His taut sculpted chest, those powerful legs and the prime everything-in-between she'd seen when the towel fell had made her melt from the inside out.

Good grief, you'd think she had never seen a naked man, she thought as she got ready for bed. Working the emergency room as she did, she'd seen dozens. So what? The sight of Mr. Gage Naked Parrish shouldn't have affected her as much as it had, but when he lost that flimsy covering, she'd nearly been affected right off her feet. She wanted to touch him, rub up against him.

She stifled a groan and squeezed her eyes shut tight, wishing the image away. Trying to focus on something else, she thought back over what she knew of his sudden reappearance in her life. Not enough, that was for sure. She'd had to bite her tongue more than once to keep from asking further questions about the GSW, his insistence on not calling the police.

Meredith resented that she was so curious, that she still cared so much. She was thrilled he was alive, overjoyed for his grandparents, but that didn't mean she wanted to be with him again. She should be glad he was leaving. She *was* glad.

Repeating that over and over in her mind, she climbed into bed. Only to be jerked awake sometime later by a harsh shout. A door slammed against the wall.

In the shifting pattern of shadows and dim light, she

saw two people—men—on their knees in her doorway. They jumped to their feet.

Heart hammering, she yanked open the drawer of her nightstand, reaching for her dad's loaded .22 caliber handgun. Her clammy hand closed over the grip. In a blur of movement, the person closest to her shoved the other into the hallway. A heavy thud told her the man had hit the wall. There was a masculine grunt, the sound of fist hitting flesh.

Thumbing off the safety, she rushed to the door in time to see Gage stumble into the wall. The intruder raised his arm.

Meredith caught a glint of light off the barrel of a gun aimed straight at Gage. "No!" she screamed.

Everything happened in staccato flashes. The unidentified man hesitated. Gage drove a fist into his jaw. The stranger leveled his weapon and fired. So did Meredith.

Her bullet hit him in the back. He jerked, his gun discharging into the bedroom beyond as he fell face-first to the floor. The man didn't move. Gage kicked the gun away then braced his good elbow against the wall, steadying himself. In the grim light, his eyes glittered like polished steel.

"Gage?" On shaking legs, Meredith stepped into the hall. "Are you okay?"

"Yeah. You?"

She nodded. Sweat slicked her palms. The smell of gunpowder burned the air as she stared at the darkly clothed motionless body. Nausea churned in her gut. "He's dead."

"Yeah." He was breathing hard, just as she was.

Jittery and trembling, she caught a movement from the corner of her eye and swung toward it. The living-room lamp provided a soft glow into the kitchen and Meredith saw a short Hispanic man at the corner, looking down the hall. Aiming a gun at them.

She froze in shock as he fired. Gage threw himself at her, knocking her back into her room. They both grunted when they hit the floor.

"Stay here." He pried the .22 from her hand, belly-crawling to the doorway.

Gage fired at the man. Two more shots sounded. Bullets struck the door frame, spraying slivers of wood. Fear had her muscles drawn taut. Dazed, Meredith curled into herself, struggling to breathe, to make sense of what was going on.

More gunfire. Another round zipped past and hit somewhere she couldn't see.

Gage got off three shots, then Meredith heard… quiet. An engine revved, then the sound grew faint. Silence closed in on them, abrupt and almost disorient-ing after the rapid-fire bursts of noise. For a long moment, all she heard was her and Gage's labored breathing.

Heart racing uncontrollably, she lay on her side, her chest aching. She wondered if her ribs were bruised. What had just happened? That man had tried to kill her. He might have succeeded if Gage's shots hadn't sent him running.

On a groan, Gage risked a look around the door frame, then straightened. "I'm going to make sure he's gone, see if anyone else is here. Got another clip?"

"In—in the drawer," she stammered.

He took the ammunition and disappeared. She told herself to move, to go to the bedroom's doorway to see if someone else *was* there. Mind numb, she managed to stand, but couldn't feel her legs. Still, she made it to the door. Long drawn out seconds raked at her nerves. Where was he? Was he okay?

She flinched when she heard the faint sound of the front door closing, then saw him move back into the kitchen and start down the hall toward her.

"He's gone. There's no one else here."

She tried to answer, but she couldn't get a breath.

"Meredith?"

Tears filled her eyes. Reaction, she knew. She sagged into the doorjamb.

"Baby?" He halted in front of her, flicking on her gun's safety and reaching around behind her to lay it on the dresser. Looking panicked, he cupped her face. "Talk to me! Are you hit?"

"No." She shook her head, managing to speak around a painful knot in her throat. Her lungs burned. She kept seeing herself shoot that man.

Gage's thumbs stroked her cheeks as he tilted her face to his. Even in the darkness, she could see the concern in his eyes. And anger. "Tell me you're all right."

"I am. I'm fine." Her body began to quiver.

Relief softening his features, he rested his forehead against hers. There was a faint trembling in his hands as he smoothed them over her hair, then her shoulders, down her sides, caressing the length of her body as if he didn't believe she was in one piece.

"I'm okay, Gage." She caught his hands at her waist. Her nerves were humming and his touch only magnified the sharp stinging sensation beneath her skin. "Just…had the wind knocked out of me."

He squeezed her fingers. "I'm sorry."

"For what? Saving my life?" She laughed weakly, struggling to regain her composure.

His face hardened. After another long look at her, he pulled away and reached over her shoulder to flip on the bedroom light. He cupped her elbow, his eyes cold and savage in a way she'd never seen. He looked…intimidating.

His gaze swept her from head to toe, taking in her pink cotton pajama top and leopard-print pants. "You sure you're okay?"

"Yes." Dazed, she stared down at the dead man lying a few feet away. She had killed him. Her, Meredith Boren.

Gage cursed. "He found me quicker than I thought he could."

"What! You know him?" Her stunned mind struggled to sort things out. Then she understood. "He's the man who shot you."

"Yes."

"Oh, my gosh!" She thought her knees might buckle. Backing into the edge of the dresser, she stared at Gage. "I killed him."

"It's a good thing you did or I'd be dead. For real." As if he couldn't help touching her, he stroked her arm, then her hair.

Her heart still pounded frantically. "I didn't hear anything until you knocked him down."

"I couldn't sleep. Heard a noise and saw him move into your room. I'd forgotten about your gun. Good thing your dad left it that summer there was a rash of burglaries down here."

Meredith nodded, only then noticing his shoulder. "You're bleeding!"

He glanced down. "I'm okay."

"Let me see." Taking an unsteady step toward him, she peeled the tape from the square gauze pads and removed them. Considering Gage had fought the jerk who'd broken in then tackled both the intruder and Meredith, it was no surprise his sutures had torn.

Only the top three, thank goodness, but blood welled up and tracked down his chest thicker and faster than she wanted to see. Still shaking, she took his hand and pressed it firmly against the wound. "Keep pressure on this while I get some bandages."

Shuddering, her legs wobbly, she inched past the dead man's feet and moved toward the kitchen in a fog of fear and relief. The events of the past few minutes played through her mind like a grainy film. With unsteady hands, she picked up the plastic box filled with medical supplies and returned to Gage.

He now sat on the end of the bed, his face ashen. As she went to him, she clumsily scooped her cell phone off the dresser. She dialed 9-1-1 then placed the phone between her shoulder and neck, snapping open the box of supplies.

Gage worked the phone away from her and disconnected. "You can't call 9-1-1."

"That man is dead!"

"You can't call anyone."

Meredith had never heard his voice flat and hard like that. The reality of everything began to sink in—his showing up here, the dead man just outside her room, bullet holes in the walls. She'd killed a man.

Suddenly light-headed, she thought she might have to sit beside Gage on the bed. "What am I supposed to do about him?"

"It'll be all right. It was self-defense."

"Who will know that?" Her voice rose. "Who will believe us?"

"Listen." Gage held her at the waist. "The AG knows what's going on. I used your cell phone this morning and let him know about the marshal trying to kill me a couple of days ago as well as you treating my gunshot wound. When we get away from here, I'll call him and tell him about the shooting. He'll take care of the body, everything."

"But—"

"It'll be okay. I promise."

She wanted to believe him. If the government could fake Gage's death, they could hide a real one, couldn't they?

Still she couldn't stop a shudder. The shooting looped over and over in her mind. She knew she'd had no choice. She hadn't shot to kill; she'd shot to protect. And if she hadn't, Gage would be dead.

"Meredith." The urgency in his voice snapped her focus back to him, what needed to be done.

Still woozy, she pushed his hand away from the wound and covered it herself. She pressed hard in an effort to staunch the bleeding and also to stop her hands from trembling. After a long moment of firm pressure, the blood flow slowed.

Hands still unsteady, she began to carefully clean the injury. He hissed out a curse, but didn't move. Adrenaline drained out of her, making her feel weak and slightly nauseous. A cold sweat covered her whole body. Once she was satisfied the bleeding had stopped, she placed a clean gauze pad over the reopened part of the wound. "Keep pressure on this and tell me what's going on. Who's that man?"

"Marshal Ed Nowlin." Gage's lips twisted. "He was assigned to me. Until two days ago, I trusted him."

Her eyes met his, silently urging him on.

"I heard him on the phone. The person on the other end found his elderly mother and was threatening to kill her unless he agreed to kill me."

She drew in a sharp breath, barely aware she was stroking his shoulder. "Who was on the phone? How did they know Nowlin was the marshal assigned to you?"

"Nowlin accused the caller of bribing someone to hack into the marshals' database. He was probably right. All the hacker had to do was find the files listing the marshals on this case and the witnesses assigned to them."

Gage's mind was stuck on the second man who'd shown up in Meredith's house and shot at them. From the statements of the men in prison, Gage was almost sure the man was Julio, the go-between who worked for the mastermind behind the arson plot. "I grabbed Nowlin's car keys, then tried to slip out the back bedroom window."

"That's when he shot you."

"Yeah. I managed to get away in his car and went to the garage where I work. I took his laptop and switched vehicles to the SUV I drove here."

Meredith's lips were tight and Gage wondered if it was because of what had just happened or because they were talking about the case that had been the last straw for them. She'd made no secret of her resentment about that.

"My plan was to go to the State Attorney General in Oklahoma City, but I knew I couldn't drive for five-plus hours. I was losing too much blood."

"So you came here for medical supplies."

He nodded, regretting that decision more every second.

"How did he find you?"

"My guess is he went to Oklahoma City first. When he couldn't find me with my grandparents or at a hospital, he probably checked your house. Once he figured out you weren't home, he would've called your hospital and learned you were out on vacation."

"But no one at the hospital would've told him where I went."

Gage could blame himself for the man finding them. "I talked about you and this place to Nowlin, told him we used to spend time here. This was probably his only lead so he drove down here. He must've run a property search to find this house."

Her face was carefully blank. He couldn't tell what she was thinking.

"Who was the other man?" She shuddered. "The Hispanic man?"

"I think his name is Julio and he works for whoever's

behind the arson ring. Each of the coconspirators stated they only ever met with a man matching his description to contract for the arsons and receive their cut of the money once the job was done. My surviving Nowlin's murder attempt must've prompted Julio's boss to send him with the marshal and make sure he killed me."

She was silent for a moment. "Who is Julio's boss?"

"I can't prove it, but I think it's a man named Larry James. He was a fire investigator, terminated for—"

"I remember. He was suspected of selling drugs, but it couldn't be proven. He was fired for bad job performance or something like that. It was all over the news because he took it to arbitration and lost."

"Yeah. Since I could never isolate the flammable material common to all the fires, the task force couldn't identify the torch or the person pulling the strings on the fire-for-hire plot. All of us working Operation Smoke Screen thought the suspects would give up a name once they were indicted, but we finally had to accept that none of them knew the identity of the mastermind. None of them ever met with anyone except the Hispanic man."

"So if Larry James is the one behind the arson ring, he did it for revenge?"

Gage nodded. "And he got it. He pushed money at the very men who cost him his job then turned them in."

"They must've gotten involved with him because they didn't know he was the same guy they'd gotten fired."

"Right. I've always thought the anonymous tip we received right before we made our arrests was from him, but like everything else about him, I can't prove it."

"Did those indicted men get involved in the arson ring because of greed?"

"Maybe one, but the others really needed the money. One to pay off a large debt, one to provide twenty-four-hour care for his elderly mother, one to pay for intensive care for his premature baby. Stuff like that."

"James involved those men, then exposed them? That's cold."

"Yeah," he said grimly. "He's ruthless and if my suspicions about Julio are right, Larry James is going to know you're with me. We have to get out of here."

"Look at you! You can't go anywhere yet."

"The SOB who ran out of here saw you. We can't stay."

She opened her mouth. To argue, he knew. He jumped in first. "Describe him to me."

She blinked. "What?"

"The bastard who shot at you. Tell me what he looks like."

She barely hesitated, though her voice shook. "Shorter than me, about five foot six. Hispanic features, baggy sweatshirt and jeans. The sweatshirt was red, I think. The lamp in the living room was on, but I couldn't see a lot of detail. There was something shiny around his neck, some kind of chain."

The more she related, the more ill Gage felt. "You saw him well enough to probably ID him. And *he* saw *you*."

Alarm widened her blue eyes. Gage wanted to hit something. Someone. He'd put her right in the line of fire, could've gotten her killed. "We have to go."

"But—"

"We can't stay, baby. He could come back and he

might not be alone next time." Gage saw anxiety cross her face, then heat spark in her eyes. She was angry at him. He didn't blame her.

She reached into the box for the sutures. "I want to know everything."

"I said I'd tell you, and I will, but not now." He noted she hadn't regained her color; her pulse still fluttered rapidly in her throat. "Get your things together and let's go."

"Let me patch you up first. That wound needs to be closed."

"There's no time for that." Her reluctance, the uncertainty in her face tugged at him and he softened his voice. "I know you want to think this through. You always do. But you'll have to trust me."

The look she gave him could've withered steel. She was already picking up another bandage. "It won't take long."

"The bleeding's nearly stopped, anyway," he said impatiently.

Her jaw firmed. "I'll butterfly it."

Knowing it would take less time to let her do it than to argue with her about it, he agreed. Maybe the task would help calm them both. Urgency pounded through him as she carefully applied the winged bandage. Gage's gut knotted when he noticed that her hands still trembled and she hadn't regained her color. They needed to get out of here.

Meredith glanced toward the marshal's body and Gage turned his head to look, too. His warm breath tickled the inside of her arm. She barely registered the shiver that rippled through her and the sudden tightness of her nipples.

Was this really happening? She'd been asking herself that about one thing or another since seeing Gage again.

"We have to go, Meredith. Right now, the only thing that matters is getting you out of here, so move it."

She bristled, but the increasing strain in his voice and the grim look in his eyes kept her quiet. She finished with his shoulder and snapped the plastic box shut, feeling as if she'd stepped outside of herself. After tossing all her clothes, her makeup case and her hair dryer into a soft-sided leather bag, she shoved his T-shirts and boxers into a tote.

His injured arm was useless so she had to help him put on his jeans and shoes. Which almost used up the last of her calm and took twice as long as it should have because she couldn't stop quivering. She felt as if she were breaking apart, piece by piece. Though she hated to admit it, she wanted to curl up next to him and pretend this wasn't happening. "Where are we going?"

"Somewhere not connected to you or your family. Maybe to the other side of the lake."

"I know a couple with a place across the highway. They winter in Florida."

"Across the highway? Back in all those trees where people rent out trailers and cabins for vacationers?"

She nodded, her chest tight because she still couldn't get a full breath. "The place I'm thinking of is a cabin, owned by the Greens. They keep the utilities on in the winter so the pipes won't freeze. I'm sure they wouldn't mind us staying there for a bit."

He'd met the retired schoolteachers at one of the Borens' summer cookouts. He rose and picked up both bags in his good hand. "All right."

"I'm bringing the medical kit, too."

He nodded and led the way out of the room. She could tell by the intent look on his face that his mind had shifted completely away from her. Well, some things never changed.

Flipping off the light, Meredith glanced one last time at the bloody, motionless man on the floor. She stared at him in disbelief as fear skittered up her spine. Dead people were no rarity in her line of work, but she'd never been the one who'd gotten them that way. She followed Gage to the unlit kitchen, waiting as he stared out the window over the sink, scrutinizing the dark. After a moment, they continued to the garage.

His shoulder had to hurt and she was concerned about renewed bleeding.

Focus on his care, she told herself. Not the dead man in your hallway.

"I'll drive." After turning on the garage light, she opened the back passenger-side door of the silver SUV with a crumpled front fender and motioned him inside. "You need to lie down. I'll get our coats, the food I brought and a couple of blankets for you."

He frowned, angling his body so that she was caught against the door, surrounded by his heat. Blue eyes glittered down at her, fully aware of her now. "I don't want you to drive. If that guy is tailing us, he'll see you. He might shoot."

"Well, I don't want to do any of this, but if he is following us, he'll shoot regardless of who's driving. I've spent every summer of my life down here and I know this area well enough that I can drive the back roads without my lights if I have to. A stranger to the area won't be able to keep up."

The tic of his jaw told her he didn't like the idea, but it made sense. Even though she knew he wouldn't let her drive solely because it was best for his injury, she added anyway, "You need to be as still as possible. The best thing for you is to take the backseat."

When he nodded curtly in agreement, she gave an inward sigh of relief.

"I'll keep an eye out for a tail." He ducked his head, slowly lowering himself onto the edge of the leather seat. His knees still outside, he curved a hand around her hip, startling her. She had no time to brace herself for the current of energy that zinged to her toes. She told herself it was the stress of the situation that had her pulse going haywire, not the man she'd nearly married.

His fingers flexed on her flesh. "I'm sorry about this. The last thing I wanted was for you to be involved." His eyes were dark, tortured. "But you're in this as deep as I am now."

She said nothing. What was there to say? That *he* made her as nervous as what had just happened?

He was her patient and as a doctor, she should've had no problem being with him, but as a woman who'd been in love with him, she had a big problem.

Right now, all she could do was put one foot in front of the other. She returned with the blankets and coats as well as the food she'd brought here. Who knew how long they'd have to stay at the Greens'?

Meredith was relieved to see Gage was inside the car and lying on his good side, facing front. His knees were bent because he was too tall to stretch out. Once she was behind the steering wheel, she adjusted the seat to give him more room. And to give herself another moment to deal with the emotion churning inside her.

She shook so hard, it took two tries to get the key in the ignition. Then her hands wrapped tightly around the steering wheel.

She'd come here to say goodbye to a man she thought was dead. Instead, she'd learned he was very much alive and there was no goodbye in sight.

Chapter 4

He was in bed with Meredith and it wasn't a dream.

In the first wash of daylight, Gage looked across the king-size mattress. There she was, closer than he'd had her in eighteen months. She slept on her back, one arm resting on her forehead, blond curls spread across the pillow. The hem of the dark green long-sleeved shirt she'd thrown on when they'd left her family's lake house rode up enough to bare a thin strip of creamy flesh.

He remembered fighting to stay alert as they'd driven across Highway 259 and weaved along the twisting roads in the heavily forested area. They hadn't been followed. Meredith had parked behind the Greens' secluded cabin, then searched for a key. She'd found it inside the porch light fixture.

The last thing he remembered was her taking off his

shirt and restitching him. He still wore his jeans. There was no memory of her getting into bed with him.

He was going to enjoy it as long as possible, since it might not happen again. Inhaling her subtle apricot scent, he rolled over on his good side to study her.

He watched the rise and fall of her breasts beneath her shirt. An extra blanket she'd found was a soft mound of yellow bunched at her waist. Very carefully, he inched over until he could skim his fingers over her sunshine hair. His injured shoulder throbbed, but it didn't matter. He itched to touch her cream-and-rose skin, stroke the fine bones of her cheeks and jaw. The elegant line of her nose. Her lips.

Thick dark lashes lay against her cheeks. He wanted to see her eyes. He wanted to see all of her. Peel away the covers and find out if she had on her jeans or only panties. Just look.

His gaze rose again to her face as he propped himself up on one elbow.

She stirred, shifting on her side to face him. Her eyes were still closed. The unguarded vulnerability on her face had a sudden fierce protectiveness welling inside him. As well as the regret he'd lived with for the past year.

He rolled to his back, then carefully sat up and got his feet on the floor. His hands clamped on to the mattress as weakness swept through him and he bowed his head. Silently, he cursed himself up one side and down the other for involving her.

He hadn't done it on purpose, but that didn't mean she was in any less danger. He couldn't let anything happen to her. He wouldn't.

"Gage?" she said in her smoke-and-velvet voice.

He looked over his shoulder, his entire body going tight at the sight of her tousled hair and sleepy blue eyes.

"Are you okay? Do you need some ibuprofen?"

"I'm fine." The pain helped dull the want burning in his belly. A little.

In the growing light, he searched her face. The warm flush on her cheeks and the fall of unruly curls brought to mind all the mornings he'd woken to see her looking just like this. The way she used to look at him before they had split up.

Her eyes were that clear endless blue he wanted to drown in, and a wave of longing hit him. Just the sight of her put a hard throb in his blood. And the dreamy way she stared at him, as if she hadn't yet remembered why they were together, what he'd done, unraveled every reason he had to keep his hands off her.

He wanted to pull her across the bed and bury his face in her hair. Kiss her sweet, warm neck. Taste her delicate skin. Her lips. He wanted to get his mouth on her. He didn't care where.

There was about as much chance of that happening as there was of no wind in Oklahoma. Furious that things had come to this, he was unable to stop the roughness in his voice. "Why don't you shower and I'll see if I can find something for breakfast?"

At his tone, the drowsiness faded from her eyes. She stiffened. "I should look at your shoulder first."

"It's fine. You can check me before I clean up, when you put something over my bandage to keep it dry."

She sat up and shoved her silky hair back out of her face with both hands. "All right. I won't be long."

He faced front, staring down at the floor, staying put until he felt her get out of bed and heard her close the door to the small bathroom behind him.

He might've lost a lot of blood, but his body still responded to her and he couldn't have hidden it. Once she was out of the room, he carefully pulled on the denim shirt he'd borrowed from her brother and moved over to the window adjacent to the bathroom door.

His SUV sat undisturbed where Meredith had left it under a winter-stripped oak. The pines and cedars were a vivid burst of green in the midst of the gray-and-white landscape. Frost glittered on the windshield and windows, covered the branch-strewn ground. There was no sign anyone had been out there.

After snagging Meredith's cell phone, Gage made his way to the front of the cabin. This place was smaller than the Borens' lake house, but comfortable. Besides the one bedroom, there was a black-and-white kitchen with sparkling appliances, glowing wood floors and a red front door with tall narrow windows on either side. The living area was small, with a red leather sofa and overstuffed chair grouped around a rock fireplace. So much for Meredith sharing a bed with him because she wanted to. Apparently, there was nowhere else for her to sleep.

Gage kept to the side of the window until he'd checked the front porch and copse of trees on both sides of the house. He saw no one.

The place was secluded and Meredith had said the neighbors to the right used their cabin only in the summer. She wasn't sure about the neighbors on their other side. Both houses were about two hundred yards away from the Greens' cabin. The gravel road leading to the porch gave a clear view of anyone approaching from the front.

Satisfied for the moment that the Hispanic man hadn't found them, Gage called Ken Ivory again. Last night, Gage had told the State Attorney General the bare bones of what had happened at Meredith's lake house. Ivory had offered to send protection, but Gage objected, saying it could draw attention to where he and Meredith were. Not to mention that he feared someone like Julio could be working in Ivory's office or watching every move the man made. Gage had been relieved when the AG said he would handle the incident discreetly.

Nowlin's body had been moved and no local law enforcement involved. After answering a spate of questions and asking some of his own, Gage hung up and opened the plastic bag of food Meredith had brought. There were two giant cinnamon bagels—her favorite— a half loaf of bread, coffee, chili, soup and crackers. He started the coffee and turned on the oven to toast the bagels about the same time he heard the creak of pipes in the bathroom, the faint rush of water.

It took zero imagination for him to picture her in the shower. His mind jumped straight to memories of water sluicing over her full pink-tipped breasts, down her sleek belly and legs. His hands would follow, then his mouth.

He narrowly missed slicing the tip of his finger with the knife he used to halve the bagels. Remembering was the worst thing he could do and not only because it might cost him more blood.

Several minutes later, she walked into the kitchen, shaking her hair free from a loose knot she'd piled on her head. She eased to the side of the front windows, checking outside the way Gage had. Good.

Turning, she padded toward him wearing socks, slim jeans and a thick blue sweater that made her eyes glitter like sapphires. "How's it going?"

"Found bagels and coffee." There were dark circles under her eyes. "How are you doing? About the shooting?"

"I don't know. I'm not sure how I'm supposed to be." Looking subdued, she peeked into the bag. "If we need anything, we can go into Broken Bow. We should probably get you at least a sweatshirt and another long-sleeved shirt. All you have are short-sleeved T-shirts and underwear."

"You can't go to town." The faint scents of soap and her apricot body wash teased him. Her skin glowed with a sheen of dampness. "You could easily be spotted."

Irritation crossed her face. "Right."

They sat down at the round stone-topped table to eat and silence hung heavy between them. Vibrating with regret and apology and shades of the past.

Gage had plenty of that stuff in the present, too. "I called the Attorney General and told him what happened last night. Once we get to Oklahoma City, we can give our statements, answer any questions we need to."

She swallowed visibly. "What about…the body?"

"Ken will handle it and inform all the appropriate authorities."

"I guess that includes the Marshals Service."

"Yeah. They already know their computer system was breached and Ken will let them know that the witnesses should be switched again to new handlers."

"Does that mean you'll get one, too?"

"I refused," he said tightly. He didn't trust anyone with Meredith's life. "There's no way I'm taking a chance that another marshal could be coerced into killing me. Or you."

The apprehension on her face had every muscle in his body clenching against the urge to hold her. He couldn't stop looking at her. As he studied the magnolia smoothness of her face, the gentle sweep of her jaw, he recalled the sweet taste of her skin, her mouth.

Meredith fixed him with a look over her coffee cup, making him realize he had been staring.

He wasn't apologizing, especially when he saw a delicate blush on her face and knew it was hueing her breasts, too.

Her eyes went frosty. "You said you'd fill me in on what was going on."

As much as he hated it, she deserved to know what they were up against.

Shoulders tense, he explained in detail how he'd come to be shot and had escaped by taking the marshal's car. How he had then exchanged the sedan for his SUV at the automobile garage where he worked. "The laptop I have is Nowlin's. When I switched cars, I took it, hoping to find something on there about who wants me killed. I haven't found anything like that yet, but when I was looking around on it yesterday, I came across a schematic of a ventilation system."

She frowned. "All the fires associated with that arson ring started in ventilation systems."

"Yeah." She'd kept up with the case. Interesting.

She squirmed, giving him a look that told him he was watching her too intently. Tough.

"That's too much of a coincidence. Less than two weeks before the trial starts, the marshal assigned to me is threatened and I'm nearly killed. A diagram for a ventilation system—part of the signature of the arsonist behind the fire-for-hire ring—just happens to show up on his computer? No."

"Does the diagram identify the building?"

"No, but I think it's the Oklahoma County courthouse. It's the one place where all the investigators in WitSec will meet."

"Could the drawing be of a system in another building? Could he have it for another reason?"

"What would it be?" He tore his gaze from her luscious mouth. Damn, he was pathetic. "If Nowlin got the schematic for a legitimate reason, like to plan security, why didn't he have blueprints of the whole building? There's no way this is a fluke. No, whoever threatened Nowlin is planning to do something using a ventilation system and the Oklahoma County courthouse is the logical place."

"And they're going to try and kill as many task-force members as possible," she said hoarsely. "Including you."

He wanted to deny it, wanted to reassure her. He couldn't.

If possible, her face paled even more. "Can't you tell the cops you suspect Larry James of being the person behind the arson ring and have them pick him up?"

"I've got nothing solid on him, even though I've been working on that the whole time I've been in witness protection."

"By doing what?"

"Trying to figure out the composition for an accelerant that leaves no trace after it burns." Gage attempted to focus solely on the discussion, not about putting his hands on her body. "Not in wood, fabric, cement, nothing."

"Then how do you know an accelerant's being used?"

"By the speed of the burn, the distortion of certain objects, points of origin. Someone has invented an agent that disappears. That requires extensive fire knowledge. I've tested dozens of different chemical combinations, trying to figure it out and so far, I haven't been able to."

"Would learning that help lead you to who's behind the arson ring?"

"It might point me in the right direction. As of now, it's the only possible lead I have, so I can't ignore it."

"Do you need a lab to do that?"

"No. I've been doing tests on my own and keeping notes."

"So you could work on it here."

"Yeah, but I need my notes and some photos I have that show the same burn pattern was found at all the fire scenes in question. Proof that the same accelerant was used."

One look at his face and she blew out an exasperated breath. "Let me guess. They're at your house in Texarkana and you want to go there."

He nodded. "As soon as possible."

"Of course you do," she said drily. "You've gone a whole six hours without bleeding or reopening your wound."

"Meredith, I need to do this."

"I know," she muttered. After a moment, she sighed. "Will you at least rest a little longer? You lost more blood when you fought with Nowlin last night."

"How about midafternoon?"

"All right." She leaned toward him, reaching out as if to touch his jaw, then pulling back. "You have a bruise there. Your knuckles are probably banged up, too."

He glanced down so she wouldn't see how badly he wanted her to touch him. He wanted to take her hand and kiss her palm, run his tongue across the delicate blue veins on the inside of her wrist.

She must've seen the intent on his face because her eyes narrowed and she pushed her chair away from the table. "I'll keep watch while you take a bath."

"All right." He needed to follow her lead and stick to the present. There was plenty to handle without dwelling on the gut-twisting ache he had for her. "It's less than a two-hour drive to Texarkana. I don't want you to go—"

"So, you don't need me anymore," she broke in hopefully. "I could—"

"I wasn't finished," he gritted out, irritated at how anxious she seemed to get away from him. Of course, why wouldn't she be? "I don't want you to go to Texarkana with me, but you have to. You sure as hell can't go back to your lake house or to Presley. And there's no way I'm leaving you alone. As much as you hate the idea, you're stuck with me until this is over."

He didn't like the idea much himself. Not only because he'd never forgive himself if something happened to her, but also because the longer they were together, the harder it became to keep his hands off her.

Meredith exhaled a shaky breath as she finished covering Gage's bandage and left him to take a bath. His blue eyes had been hot and intense on her. She needed some space and she wasn't going to get it anytime soon.

Stuck with him, he'd said.

Seven more days. She would be with him that long or until they got to Oklahoma City. What had started out as annoyance at his announcement had turned to panic. Because she'd spent the past thirty minutes trying to ignore his frank male appraisal. Because she'd dreamed about him. *Them.*

One night on the same mattress and boom. She couldn't remember the last time she'd dreamed about him before this. Her jaw clamped so tight she felt a twinge in her cheek. She was restless and hot and mad. She'd been that way since waking up next to him, feeling his warmth like a touch. Glimpsing the dark hunger in his eyes.

When she had climbed into bed with him last night, she knew she could be tempting herself, tempting him, but she'd done it anyway. Because there was no way she was sleeping alone after killing that man.

She was an idiot. She'd thought getting away from

her lake house and going somewhere else would be better because there would be no memories in the new place. They wouldn't be in every shadow or corner or possession she touched. But this was just as bad.

While Gage was in the bath, she cleaned bagel crumbs from the table and swept the floor. Called her parents and told them it was taking longer down here than she'd expected.

Wandering to the small living area, the quiet pulsed around her. Everything kept at bay by thoughts of Gage caught up to her—shooting the marshal, nearly being shot herself, the fear, the fight, the blood.

Just like that, tears started. She sank down onto the red leather sofa, dabbing at her eyes. A physical release of stress, she knew. But she couldn't stop. The more she swiped at her tears, the faster they flowed.

Suddenly a big warm hand covered her left one. "Meredith?"

Gage's hushed voice was soothing and she tried to check her sobs. Through blurry eyes, she saw the concern on his face.

"Nowlin?"

She nodded, tears burning her cheeks.

Warm and steady, he sat in the chair next to the sofa, loosely clasping her fingers. His knee brushed hers. After a few minutes, she had herself under control.

Still she couldn't suppress a shudder. "I shot him. I killed him." She gave a watery laugh. "Like you don't know that. I just…can't believe it happened."

Gage brushed his thumb lightly back and forth across her knuckles.

"It's only now sinking in, I guess. It's a delayed reaction. I know that, but I can't seem to help it."

"You don't have to. You've been through a lot, Meredith. Just let it out."

He didn't try to hold her or fix her, just waited patiently as more tears fell. They finally stopped. Slowly she became aware of the hum of the refrigerator, the coarse caw of a bird outside. The familiar scent of soap and man settled her.

She squeezed his hand. "Sorry."

He thumbed away a streak of wetness on her cheek. "You okay?"

"Yes," she said hoarsely. The tenderness in his eyes had her chest going tight. "It's overwhelming. I know I saved your life and I'm not sorry for that."

"Good to know," he said drily.

She smiled. "It's just…he's dead. In med school, we were taught how to deal with death, but it's different with patients. The marshal wasn't a patient."

Gage listened as she worked her way through it, keeping hold of her hand. As she calmed, she took in his damp hair, the steadiness in his hands, the hard hair-dusted chest visible between the edges of his open shirt. And the heat in his blue eyes.

His thumb softly stroked her ring finger. Had he been doing that all along? Awareness fluttered down low and she slowly slid her hand from his. "I feel better now."

About the marshal. Not about Gage.

He laughed. "You don't have to sound so surprised."

"I'm not." Her mouth curved. She had always admired his patience. Except when it came to them and the wedding he had seemed content to wait on forever.

She might not like what he'd done to them, she might not trust him with her heart, but she did trust him with her life. "I'm not sure I would be able to handle this with anyone except you. Thanks."

His gaze sharpened. Maybe she shouldn't have said that out loud, but she meant it.

Shifting closer, he rested his elbows on his thighs. "I'm glad to return the favor."

"What do you mean?" She dried the last of her tears. "Oh, saving my life after I saved yours."

"No." He shook his head, seeming to consider his words carefully. "I'm talking about the past year. Thinking about you was what got me through."

She stiffened. "Gage."

"Remembering us."

She didn't want to hear this. She couldn't. She wasn't going back. "Stop. Please."

After a long, heavy minute that had her quivering deep inside, he looked straight into her eyes. Her pulse skipped. She couldn't ignore the fierce need on his face.

"I can't stop thinking about being in bed with you this morning. And how we used to wake up. Remember?"

Oh, she remembered, all right. This was why he'd been watching her with such blatant interest all morning. "Well, we didn't wake up that way today!"

"Trust me, I know. Every part of me knows," he added wryly.

Before she could stop herself, she glanced at his

groin and her eyes widened at his unmistakable arousal.
"You can't— You're hurt!"

"I'm not dead."

Panic had her surging to her feet. She wanted to run,
but where? "Okay, listen. There's one bed in this place.
It's plenty big enough for both of us, so you better not
try anything. You've been looking at me like you want
to take a big bite."

His gaze did a slow slide down her body. "I'd be
lying if I said I didn't."

Meredith wanted to smack him. "I'm not sleeping
with you. We're not sleeping together. There will be no
sex. None."

"What about—"

"No kissing. No touching."

He arched a brow and amusement glinted in his eyes.
"I was going to say what about afterward? What about
after this is over?"

She blinked. Was he serious? Regardless of how the
trial turned out, their basic problem would still be the
same. He would always put her second to his job.
"There is no 'after this.'"

"No?"

"No."

His eyes darkened as he rose, his body almost touching hers. A frantic electric sensation screamed through
her body, zinging clear down to her toes.

She wasn't sure what she expected, but it wasn't for
him to lean close and whisper, "Whatever you say."

The soft arrogance in his voice didn't sound like
agreement to her. It sounded like a challenge.

Her pulse spiked and her nipples tightened. She shouldn't want him ever again, but she did. Meredith folded her arms, trying to look as if she were unaffected, but she could tell by the infuriating satisfaction in his eyes he'd already seen. Her entire body flushed.

Before she could step away, he did. It scared her how quickly some of her old emotions had surfaced. The anger, the regret. And the want. Especially that one.

Seven days to go before the trial. Seven days of *this*.

She mentally braced herself. Things were what they were and she had to deal with it. She could suck it up for seven days. She could do this without getting involved again.

"We can come back here after we finish in Texarkana." He skirted the leather chair and walked down the hall toward the bedroom, hopefully to rest.

As Meredith watched his slow progress, her gaze took in the stubborn set to his shoulders, the jeans she only now noticed were loose on him. She went hot, then cold. Her legs felt like rubber. Those seven days loomed before her like a long stretch of desert. She was afraid she couldn't tough it out at all.

Because she had never gotten over him.

Chapter 5

She'd said no sex, but she still wanted him. Gage had seen proof in her body. Her eyes. And he planned to get her to admit it. He was driven by ego, but he didn't care.

She hadn't wanted to hear that sometimes thoughts of her had been the only thing to keep him going. Maybe he shouldn't have confessed, but he wanted her to know how much she still meant to him.

His day had been spent sleeping off and on, and searching through more files on Nowlin's computer. Even though Gage chafed at the inactivity, he knew he had to regain his strength. And leaving Texarkana after dark was a precaution they should take.

Meredith had dodged him most of the day. She was skittish though he didn't know if it was because of what he'd admitted in the living room or because there was still a spark between them.

This morning had started a slow throb of anticipation in his blood. Knowing this might be the last chance he had to ever spend any time with her made the hunger sharper, deeper, and being with her until the trial was going to test his restraint.

His awareness of her sawed away at his control as they drove to Texarkana later that day to pick up his notes and fire-scene photos. The sun was setting in a ball of pure orange. Gage didn't mind Meredith being behind the wheel; he just wished he had something to do with his hands, his mind. Something to override the sweet scent of her wrapping around him, the memory of how she'd responded to him earlier.

Tension arced between them. Because of him, he knew. He was making her uncomfortable, but he couldn't quite bring himself to be sorry. Waking up with her this morning had done more than fire his blood. It had unlocked memories of all the mornings he'd woken with her before. And all the ones he hadn't.

He tried to think about other things, other people. Maybe the silence was getting to her as well because she slid a look at him. "How long have you worked at the car garage?"

"Since I got there last year."

"You always could fix anything," she said, her lips curving.

Not us, he thought. Her smile still pushed his buttons, made him itch to get his hands on her. Hoping to hide his reaction, he glanced out the window. He didn't want to talk about him. He wanted to know what had been going on in her life. "How are Terra and Jack?"

Presley's first female fire investigator was one of Meredith's best friends. She and her husband, Jack Spencer, had become good friends to Gage, too.

Meredith accelerated past a semitruck. "They're doing great. They have a baby now, Elise."

Gage had never thought about having babies with Meredith, but he thought about it now.

"She's a little over a year old."

"That's nice. Before I went into Witness Security, I ran into Terra at a fire investigator seminar, so I knew she was pregnant. How's Robin?"

Meredith's other close friend was a highly regarded cop on the Presley P.D.

"She's well. She's a detective now. Last year, she was hurt in a fire."

"How badly?"

"Luckily she wasn't burned. Her leg was gashed by some falling debris, badly enough to need quite a few stitches."

Gage shifted in the corner of the seat, trying to keep pressure off his injured shoulder. His gaze fixed on Meredith's face, the creamy skin he knew was velvety soft. All over. The need to touch her was even worse than it had been this morning. "She ever get married?"

"No." Meredith shook her head emphatically. "I don't think she ever will after what happened."

"Can't say I blame her. Her fiancé jilting her right before the ceremony probably doesn't make her inclined to get serious about anyone."

Meredith nodded. "It's been almost five years and she still doesn't know which of Kyle's groomsmen convinced him that she was the worst person he could marry."

"Brutal."

"It's horrid. At least that didn't happen with—"

Us. He knew what she'd been about to say. Remembering the stark pain in Meredith's eyes when they had split up, Gage figured what he had done had hurt her just as badly.

She filled the awkward pause. "Your grandparents got a new dog."

He grinned. "How does Rex like that?"

Regret flashed across her face. "Rex died about three months ago."

"Oh." The news about his bird dog jarred him. "That had to be really hard on Gramps."

She nodded. "Fifteen years is a long time to have a dog. He was a member of your family."

Gage stared out the window. Rex, gone. One more thing that had happened without Gage knowing. He and Gramps had trained the black Labrador together. The animal had been a big part of Gage's growing up. His chest felt hollow. Not only because of losing the dog, but also because of everything he'd missed.

There were chunks of his life he would never get back. People he might never see again. People he'd let down. He should've been there for his grandparents, for Meredith. Failing his grandparents could be blamed on his having to go into hiding, but not his problems with Meredith. No, he'd screwed up their relationship before his supposed death.

Talking with her, being with her, put a sharp bite in his blood. Over the past year, he'd been able to numb himself to some extent, he realized. Since seeing Meredith again, his body had been slowly unthawing. Spending time with her brought back every emotion he'd locked away—want, need, regret, loneliness. Love. He hadn't been aware of how completely he'd shut himself off. How empty he'd felt.

As they headed east, then south through Arkansas on U.S. 71, he asked questions about some of the arson cases he'd seen reported over the past few months in Presley's online newspaper. She told him Terra Spencer now had another full-time fire investigator, Collier McClain, whose first case had been a serial arsonist-killer.

They talked about changes in Presley and other friends they shared. As best she could, Meredith answered his questions about his grandparents, about Aaron and Gage's fellow fire investigators. All things he should've gotten to experience. Life—*his life*—had gone on without him. As had the woman sitting beside him.

Looking at her, aching at the memory that he hadn't been able to touch her the way he wanted this morning, he'd never felt more alone.

They reached Texarkana just after dark. Along with the notes and photos, Gage intended to pick up some clothes at his house and if they were careful, purchase anything else they needed from a store here.

So far, there had been nothing on the news about him or Meredith so Gage felt Ken Ivory was handling everything the way he'd promised.

Gage directed her to an older neighborhood of small

frame houses and had her park around the block. They walked through the field that ran behind a row of fenced backyards. This way, there was less chance of being noticed, especially by his widowed neighbor, Ralph, a former Army Ranger.

When they reached Gage's yard, he helped Meredith over the four-foot chain-link fence, catching sight of Ralph's tabby cat prowling the length of the back porch. Light from the fat white moon showed the back bedroom window through which Gage had escaped was still open. Fishing his keys out of his pocket, he opened the patio door and stepped inside.

He froze, his grip tightening on the semiautomatic he and Meredith had brought with them from her lake house. "Sonova—"

He scanned the living area. The dark tweed couch cushions were slashed, the drawers of both end tables had been yanked out and dumped, lamps broken. Shock shifted to apprehension.

"Stay here," he whispered over his shoulder. He checked the other rooms. Once convinced they were alone, he returned to Meredith. "The whole house is torn up like this."

She followed him across the living room and down a hallway littered with linens and books and papers. They passed one ransacked bedroom before reaching his. Clothes were thrown from his closet and drawers. His mattress was shoved half off the bed.

"What were they looking for?"

Unaware that she had eased up on his right side, Gage jerked toward her.

"Sorry," she breathed at his abrupt movement.

"Maybe whoever broke in was looking for my notes or photos. Maybe info on me. Hell if I know."

"Do you think it was Julio?"

"Could've been. Or Nowlin could've trashed everything before leaving here and finding us at your lake house."

Gage moved to the solid oak headboard and tried to pull it away from the wall with his left hand.

Meredith made an exasperated sound and hurried to the other side of the bed to help him.

"Thanks." Shoulder aching, he felt his way down the frame toward the lower half then pushed in on a section. A square piece popped out and Gage removed it. Anyone who didn't know about the hiding place he'd cut into the wood wouldn't notice anything unusual.

Relief pumped through him when his hand closed over the small notebook and fire-scene photos. He passed them to Meredith. "Would you hold these while I grab some clothes?"

Taking a duffel bag from his closet floor, he stuffed in sweatshirts, jeans and socks. He stepped into a small bathroom and grabbed his shaving kit. "Let's get out of here."

They left the same way they'd come, hurrying silently across the crackling winter grass and back to the SUV. The silence, the heavy chill coiled Gage's muscles tight. And it wasn't lost on him that his wrecked house mirrored the shambles his life had become.

At the edge of town, they stopped at a discount store for some clothes, then a convenience store for gas. Impatient and edgy, Gage knew he wouldn't relax until they reached the cabin. He and Meredith took turns in the restroom then she filled the gas tank. When he protested, she said, "You're moving as if you're hurt. Someone might notice that, but they won't notice me."

In an effort to hide her face in case there were working security cameras around, she wore one of Gage's baseball caps he'd found under the seat. He stayed in the SUV, scrutinizing the driver's side where she stood and the passing vehicles on the street beyond.

As they continued on their way, Gage kept watch on the highway behind them.

Features pinched with concern, Meredith glanced over. "Do you see anything suspicious?"

"Not yet."

"We weren't followed down here, so maybe we're in the clear."

"Maybe." He wasn't assuming anything.

The image of his ransacked house looped through his brain, a grim reminder of the danger they could still face.

The traffic wasn't heavy, but it was steady. When they crossed the border into Arkansas, they began to see more semitrucks than automobiles. Some truck trailers were loaded with lumber or machinery, some were empty.

Gage and Meredith made it through DeQueen, Arkansas, without spotting a tail. There was about twenty-four miles to go until Broken Bow, then another thirteen or so miles to the Greens cabin. The tight pressure across his chest eased. They would be all right.

But when they stopped at the light on Park Drive to

turn toward the lake, his attention was caught by a distinctive pair of round headlights. Exactly like some he'd seen on an older car at the convenience store in Texarkana.

As he and Meredith started out of town, Gage swore.

Her gaze jerked to him. "What? What is it?"

The vehicle held its position a few car lengths back. He touched Meredith's leg. "We're being followed."

She drew in a sharp breath, looking in the rearview mirror. "Do you think it's Julio?"

"That's a good possibility. Don't change your speed."

"Okay." Her voice was thin. "What do we do?"

Gage's hands curled into fists. He'd been vigilant about watching for anyone following them. How had the tail suddenly appeared? It didn't matter. They had to get rid of him. "We can't go back to the Greens' and I don't know if we could lose the tail in Broken Bow. The town's too small."

For a long minute, neither spoke. The silence turned heavy with apprehension.

"We need a plan B," Meredith said.

"I'm fresh out of those."

"I might have an idea." She glanced in the rearview mirror.

Gage was glad to see the tail hadn't gotten closer. "What?"

"We'll go past the lake, past Smithville and take one of the logging roads into the mountains. If the person following us manages to make it as far as the logging road, they won't make it much farther."

It was a good idea. Gage had hunted in the heavily forested area with her brothers and knew how easy it was to get lost on roads that were often no more than lumber-truck ruts. "It's really difficult to find your way out, even in the daylight."

"Not if you know where you're going."

True. Her brothers, as familiar with the area as Meredith, had managed to get in and out of their hunting camp just fine.

"All right. Let's lose him."

She nodded, her face ghost-pale in the darkness. Gage bit back a curse. He wanted to tell her everything would be okay, but as long as she was with him, it wasn't.

As they passed the lake and traffic thinned, the speed limit increased. And the car trailing them closed in. Meredith hoped she could lose him. She thought she could.

Fear was a cold lump in her throat. She focused on keeping at least one vehicle between them and their pursuer as they passed the entrance to Beavers Bend State Park, then a lake area called Stevens Gap. Meredith drew on her years of E.R. experience to stay calm when what she wanted to do was scream, pretend none of this was happening.

She thought she could hear Gage's heart pounding as loudly as hers. He kept watch out the back window while Meredith monitored the rearview mirror. In the flash of a passing semi's lights, she saw the grimness, the guilt on his face, and knew he blamed himself.

Meredith was starting to see the price he'd paid the past year, was still paying.

A road sign listed the upcoming towns of Smithville, Bethel and Battiest, then a billboard-sized sign welcomed them to the Ouachita National Forest. The highway curved and they were heading east. The moon was bright and in the distance, Meredith could see the night-draped forested mountains.

The tail still followed. Meredith accelerated, driving over the Eagle Fork Creek bridge. Hands clammy, chest tight, she drove through the small town of Watson, then turned right toward the cemetery, slowing when the road became dirt and gravel and holes. Coming to a fork in the road, she again went right.

There were huge gouges in the red dirt road, deep enough to crack teeth if they hit one going too fast. The SUV's lights were a beacon to the person behind them, but she couldn't turn them off, not yet.

The forest of trees along both sides of the road blocked most of the moonlight. Gage's vehicle bumped and rattled as the road twisted and climbed.

He spoke loud enough to be heard over the noise. "We could get lost, just like him."

"Maybe."

"I never could get my bearings when we came here to hunt."

That was because the only landmarks this far into the mountains were trees and more trees. One might be marked with a band of white or red spray paint, but the next one would be, too. "Let's hope whoever's behind us can't find their way, either."

Meredith put the SUV in four-wheel drive and started up a steep incline. She could see the car keeping pace behind her and she was nearly frantic to put more distance between them. At least that person couldn't travel any faster than her and Gage.

Deep, rock-pitted ditches ran along the road. Suddenly, she steered into one. Their vehicle bounced hard enough to slam her and Gage's heads into the ceiling. Hissing out a harsh breath, he grabbed the dash to steady himself.

"Sorry." Meredith searched for a narrow opening and took it, driving up a small rise and over felled tree limbs, decades-old cushions of pine needles and twigs, mounded mud. When the ground leveled out, she stopped, killing the lights and the engine.

Their labored breathing was loud in the abrupt silence.

The quiet was palpable. The grind of a car engine sounded over the chirps and rustles of night animals. Bright lights speared through the trees, but didn't reach them. Chest tight, Meredith fought the urge to grab hold of Gage's hand, hoping they couldn't be seen in the dense growth. The car passed, the engine's rumble faded.

Meredith and Gage stayed frozen, waiting. Soon, she heard a car coming back toward them. Was it the one that had been following them? Had they been found?

Seconds pricked her nerves like needles. When the vehicle drove past their hiding place and she saw it *was* the car that had been tailing them, she felt Gage's relief as strongly as her own.

Neither of them spoke until they could no longer

hear the automobile. He reached over and squeezed her waist. "You did it."

Tension drained out of her and she slouched down in the seat, boneless. "For a minute, I was afraid he might find us."

"Me, too." Gage looked at the surrounding woods. "Do you think we could get out of here using the other route you know?"

"Not in the dark, and we can't go back the way we came. If that guy manages to make it to the highway, he could be waiting down there."

"So…"

"So?" Meredith glanced over, realization dawning at the same moment he spoke. She opened her mouth to tell him not to say it, but he beat her to it.

"Looks like we'll be sleeping together again."

She rolled her eyes at his choice of words, while trying desperately to keep the panic off her face.

Her with Gage. In much closer quarters than a king-size bed. This morning, he'd seen how much he still affected her. She had to be careful.

It didn't take long for a chill to settle in the car and the windows to frost from their breath. They moved to the backseat and laid it flat to give them room to sleep. They traded places so Gage could rest on his good side if he wanted.

From behind the driver's seat, he broke the silence. "If we're going to be here all night, we should use the sweatshirts we bought earlier."

"Those blankets we took from the lake house are still in here, too." As he pulled the new garments out of the bag, Meredith stretched to the back corner and retrieved the blankets, passing one to him. She slipped off her coat to pull on the sweatshirt.

He tossed something soft and white at her. "I figure you're going to want a pair of these socks, too."

Despite his teasing tone, they stared at each other in tense silence. Her feet were always cold in the winter. When she and Gage had been together, she would filch a pair of his socks to wear over her own.

Judging from the knowing glitter in his eyes, he was remembering, as she was, how she would beg him to rub her feet and warm them up. She didn't want to think about their past. Spending the night with him was going to be hard enough.

Pulse hitching, she drew her blanket around her shoulders, searching for something to say, anything to prevent other reminders of their past. "You know, there are several Vietnam veterans who live up here."

After giving her a long, measuring look, Gage leaned against the back of the driver's seat. "Your brothers mentioned that the last time we were here."

"No one ever sees them. I don't know if they ever leave the mountain. It's sad and intriguing at the same time."

Sitting cross-legged at his hip, she looked past him to the window and froze. Her heart skipped as two big dark eyes stared back at her. A brown face with white circling the eyes and inside the ears identified the animal as a whitetail deer. No antlers, which meant it was a female. Her jet-black nose with two white bands behind it pressed against the glass as the doe watched them, unblinking.

Gage turned his head, following Meredith's gaze. He went still. "Wow."

"Yeah. Think she'll do anything aggressive?"

"Not if we don't."

Amazing. They sat there in breathless silence as the animal snuffled, frosting the glass, then sniffed its way down the side of the SUV. After a moment, it disappeared into the darkness.

Relaxing, Meredith blew out a breath. "That was a surprise."

"Too bad I never saw a deer that close when I was hunting with your brothers."

Meredith smiled at him, but something about his words nagged at her. Something about seeing. Then things started falling into place. The night she'd found him in her kitchen, the night Julio had shot at them before Gage saw him. Previously tonight when she had come up beside him in his bedroom, startling him. And just now.

Given where the deer had stood, Gage should've seen the animal from the corner of his eye. And he hadn't. He should've seen all those earlier things when she had, if not before.

"You have no peripheral vision on your right side," she said slowly, certainly. "Why?"

She thought he might have winced. He opened another plastic sack and dug out a box of granola bars. "Hungry?"

"There are only a couple of ways that can happen. One is disease and the other is blunt-force trauma." She was afraid she knew which it was. Her heart started pounding hard. "Tell me."

"I'm fine."

She felt his reluctance like a wall. "You told me there were two attempts on your life. That was why you had to go into Witness Security, why you had to fake your death."

He stared straight ahead, his face stone-hard in the shadowy light.

"Gage." She heard the plea in her voice; she had to know. "They nearly killed you."

"Yes," he confirmed grudgingly. "Once with a gun, once with a baseball bat and a pipe. The bullets missed, but—"

"You were beaten horribly. That's what happened."

He dragged a hand down his face. "I'm fine now."

"Tell me what they did to you."

"Baby, we don't have to talk about this."

She scooted closer until her knees touched his thighs. She wanted him to look at her. Her voice shook. "I need to know."

After a long minute, he answered. "Broke two ribs, my jaw, my nose."

"And damaged your orbital rim."

He nodded.

She swallowed hard. Something inside her went dark and flat. For the first time, she *felt* how close he'd come to being killed. The realization was a razor-sharp slice through her heart.

Finally, his gaze met hers. "I'm okay."

She rose to her knees, the blanket sliding off her shoulders. With a trembling hand, she reached out and feathered her fingertip against the corner of his eye.

He froze. She shouldn't be touching him. Since waking up with her this morning, his body had been humming with tension. He closed his eyes, just for a moment, savoring her silky soft touch against his temple.

All the need he'd tried to smother the past year crashed over him. Gage couldn't help pressing into her touch.

Her hand on his face, the naked emotion in her eyes, her faint apricot scent. She was *right there,* her breath caressing his skin. All he had to do was shift, so he did.

His lips brushed hers, lingered. She stiffened. He waited for her to push him away. Instead, her mouth settled against his and a breathless broken sound came from her throat.

Driven purely by the hot slide of her mouth, Gage teased her lips open, trying to rein in the urge to drag her into his lap, bury himself in her.

He was shaking, unable to believe she wasn't fighting him. She tasted like every good thing he'd lost.

His heart nearly stopped when her arms crept around his neck. She was trembling, just as he was. He was starving for her. He told himself to go slow, savor the honeyed heat of her mouth, but he'd wanted her too long, missed her too much.

Still, he managed some control until she pressed hard against him and he felt the fullness of her breasts through her sweater and sweatshirt. He nearly lost it.

His hands cupped her skull and he ate at her mouth. Selfishly, greedily taking what he could get, knowing that any second she would pull away.

And she did.

Breathing hard, she placed her hands on his shoulders and held him back. "No," she panted. "Stop."

Yes, she was calling a halt, but for the first time since Gage had found her at the lake house, hope flared that she might give them another chance.

She must've seen it on his face. Shaking her head, she moved away. The dreamy desire in her eyes shifted to regret, then a cool remoteness. "No. We're over. I can't be with you."

"Even after the trial?" His body ached for her. He literally hurt deep down in his gut.

"The trial has nothing to do with us. We didn't end our relationship because of Operation Smoke Screen. It wasn't the reason things went wrong between us. It was just the last straw. I couldn't be second to your job anymore."

We hadn't ended their relationship. *She* had.

"You still want me."

"It doesn't matter."

"Baby—"

"I won't let you hurt me again," she whispered.

The way she was hurting him now. And it did hurt. He knew she had no reason to trust he wouldn't screw things up again, but that didn't stop the flash of anger he felt at himself, at her, the whole situation.

"Don't…kiss me again."

He wanted to point out that while he may have started it, she'd done as much as he had, but he bit back the words. Curling his hands into fists, he managed to keep from reaching for her.

As she edged away, he had the insane impulse to

keep kissing her until she changed her mind. There was no way in hell that would turn out well.

He'd hurt her too much and evidently he'd be paying for that jackass mistake the rest of his life. No matter how badly he wanted her, pressuring her about it was selfish. He couldn't do it, even though he knew she still felt something for him.

This time, maybe their last time together, had to be all about what she needed. He didn't want to hurt her anymore.

Chapter 6

Gage stayed where he was, leaning back against the driver's side seat, knees bent. He was rock-hard and it took a couple of minutes for his blood to cool. Frost filmed the windows of the SUV. Wrapped in the blanket Meredith had given him, his warm breath puffing out into the frigid air, he could still feel the hot slide of her mouth against his. The freezing temperature didn't do a thing to douse the burn she'd started in his body.

She lay a foot away, huddled in a ball under her blanket. In the darkness, he caught the occasional glimpse of her pale hair above the blanket, the white of her socks and part of her shoes sticking out the bottom. If there had been enough light, Gage knew he would've been able to see that her lips were blue. She shifted, turned, wrapped her feet in the blanket for the third time.

Neither of them would get any sleep like this.

He'd already dug a hole with her so he went ahead and dug it deeper. "We need to huddle together, Meredith."

He waited. One, two—

She rolled toward him, peeking over the edge of her blanket. *"What?"*

"It's really cold in here." The chill bored into his shoulder like a drill. "I think we can handle combining our body heat for one night. At least, *I* can."

He'd known that would get her. The sharp look she gave him pierced through the thick darkness like a blade. She sat up slowly, the shadows of the night shifting around her.

"If you're worried about me getting off on it, don't be." *He* would have to worry about it, but she wouldn't.

"I'm not worried about…that."

Even though he couldn't see her very well, he felt her gaze drop to his lap. All his nerve endings popped and his body clenched. Damn. "I got the message a while ago, Meredith. You're not interested in picking up where we left off."

"That's right."

Did she have to sound so certain about it? "We proved this morning we can sleep in the same bed without me jumping you. I want you, Meredith, but I do understand the word *no*."

"I know that." She sounded defensive.

"Okay, then."

She hesitated, which pissed him off. What did she think he was going to do? Tear off her clothes and start in on her?

"Yes or no?" he snapped.

"Yes, but I'll sleep behind you."

"Whatever," he muttered.

She crawled around him as he scooted to the middle of the vehicle. After he arranged his blanket beneath them, Meredith helped smooth it out then handed over their only pillow as she lay down.

Once she was on her side facing him, he settled the other covering over them, tucking it around her feet before he turned his back to her and stretched out as best he could on his left side.

They both ducked their heads beneath the blanket to trap as much heat inside their makeshift cocoon as possible. Behind him, she was as stiff as a rail.

The cold sank down around them one numbing layer at a time. Meredith had been taking care of him since he'd arrived. He would like to do the same for her once.

He caught the scent of her fragrant skin, her shampoo. "Better?" he asked quietly.

"Yes, thanks." Her voice was muffled, her breath a hot puff through his shirt.

She still hadn't relaxed. The only way she would was if he showed her she didn't need to worry about something happening between them.

"I'm going to sleep now, so don't try anything."

He felt more than heard her soft laugh at his teasing. After a few long moments, their breathing leveled out. Gage's muscles began to warm. Meredith burrowed into him. She had to be asleep or she wouldn't have done it.

Her cheek lay flat between his shoulder blades, her

breasts burned into his back. The cradle of her thighs held him tight.

Like a short-circuited screen, images flashed through his brain of them naked. His hands on her, in her. His mouth, too. Over and over and over.

Excellent idea, Parrish. You idiot. Finally, he could feel his toes again, his fingers. And every inch of Meredith.

Since forsaking his old life, he'd dealt with only memories, but this was her in the flesh. *Her* flesh against *his*.

Warm breath whispered past his ear. Her hair tickled the back of his neck. The sweet woman scent of her settled in his lungs. She shifted, her arm sliding over his hip and he ground his teeth. He wanted to reach for her, curve his hand around the back of her thigh and lock her to him, but he didn't.

He wanted her body, but he wanted her trust more.

He was going to keep his word, even though she had just kissed him as if she wanted to crawl inside him. He could handle this. He *would* handle it.

He'd have a lot more confidence in that if he hadn't been dreaming for the past year about having her right up against him.

When early morning light filtered into the SUV, Meredith came awake, toasty-warm, her cheek pressed against Gage's shoulder blade. Except for the occasional rustle of an animal outside, all was quiet. Meredith registered that her right hand lay flat against Gage's hard belly. As if she were holding him to her. Even beneath two shirts, she could feel the muscles of his abdomen. His heat pulsed against her like a furnace.

Cold air stung her ear and the side of her face. A thick frost covered all the windows.

Still half-asleep, she wanted to slide her hands under his clothes and rub against his hot bare flesh, stroke her hands across his chest, his stomach. Lower.

The fierce want startled her out of her drowsiness. After she'd told him there would be no touching, she was stuck to him like varnish on a dresser.

She could tell by Gage's utter stillness that he was awake, too. Great.

Before she could move, his body coiled tighter against hers. He shifted, his backside brushing against her and causing a tickle of warmth low in her belly.

"Morning." The word came out grainy, velvet-rough.

His deep slumberous voice stroked over her like a touch and triggered memories she didn't want. Meredith squeezed her eyes shut. "Good morning."

She sounded breathless and a strange urgency hammered through her. For cryin' out loud!

She'd told him no touching, no kissing and last night, they'd done both. She might have been unaware of putting her arm around him while asleep, but she had gone into that kiss knowing full well what she was doing. Despite telling herself to pull away the instant she'd seen the intent in his face, she hadn't been able to make herself move. She'd looked in his eyes and her stomach had tumbled, just like the first time he'd kissed her.

So far, she'd done everything she'd told him *not* to

do. Irritated, she dragged her hand off him and scooted back, huddling inside her coat, which she'd slept in.

He sat up, scrubbing a hand down his face. "Did you get any sleep?"

"Yes." The frigid air had goose bumps breaking out all over her body as she came up on her elbow.

Half expecting him to gloat over the fact that he'd kept his hands to himself and she hadn't, she couldn't look at him. Meredith pulled her coat tighter around her.

They climbed out and quietly checked the area then scraped the frost from the windows as best they could. She knew Gage was as relieved as she was when they discovered they were alone. The quiet around them made Meredith fairly certain there were no other vehicles nearby.

Feeling it was safe enough, Meredith started the car and turned on the heater. They waited only a couple of minutes before slowly forging their way out the other side of the thick woods. Getting through and around the crowded trees, and over mounds of packed dirt and twigs required all of her concentration.

At some point, she stopped expecting Gage to taunt her about draping herself all over him. She certainly wasn't going to mention it.

Descending the twisting, steep roads down the back side of the mountain took over an hour. Then another hour to circle around and reach the highway a few miles south of where they had turned off it last night. There was no sign of anyone following or posted near the highway, watching for them. If the person who had tailed them was waiting, he was probably north of them, close to where they'd left the highway to take the road leading to Watson.

Once Gage and Meredith were back at the cabin, they carried in the things they'd picked up in Texarkana.

He'd been quiet during their drive, but when he walked past her into the cabin, admiration glinted in his eyes. "That was some slick driving, Doc. Good hiding place."

"Thanks." She didn't want to admit how his praise warmed her. "Growing up, I never thought I'd have to go up there to lose a tail."

They left the blankets and pillow in the SUV. While Gage put away his small suitcase and shaving kit, Meredith heated up chili for lunch. After eating, she checked Gage's wound and put on a fresh bandage. She showered, then he did.

They were both quiet throughout the day. Restless and frustrated about waking up all over him, Meredith wanted more than the space of one room between them, but she wasn't going to get it anytime soon. She started a load of laundry and tried to take a nap.

Gage sat at the round kitchen table with his notebook and the dead marshal's laptop. Meredith finished folding and putting away the laundry, wondering how long they would be here.

Gage was completely, totally focused on his notes, seemingly unaware of anything else. Of her. How irritating. And familiar.

Turning off all but the kitchen light, Meredith made her way into the living area. She discovered the fireplace in the corner burned on fake logs, not real wood.

They could have a fire without having to worry about smoke from the chimney.

She settled on the red leather sofa and turned on the television to watch the news, relieved when there was no mention of a dead marshal, protected witnesses, Gage or her. An image of Nowlin lying dead in her hall blazed across her mind.

Since shooting him, she thought about it frequently and would for a long time to come. But she didn't want to think about it now. She didn't want to think about anything although she couldn't stop her thoughts from going to the big man at the table behind her. Or that panty-melting kiss they'd shared. Or waking up this morning draped over him like a blanket.

Across the few feet separating them, Meredith caught his woodsy masculine scent. Shoulders angled into the corner of the sofa, she propped her head on her fist and tried to watch a late-night talk show, but her gaze kept sliding to Gage.

To look at him, one would think the only thing on his mind was his notebook. Meredith wished her thoughts would go to something else, but watching him made her think about that kiss, want more. And regret it at the same time.

She itched to offer any help she could, but she stubbornly, selfishly wanted to keep her distance from him. Especially since he acted as if last night had never happened.

That stung, she admitted grudgingly. How could their kiss be so easy for him to dismiss?

Finally, she gave up trying not to look at him. He wasn't aware of her, so she could look all she wanted.

In the white light of the fixture hanging over the kitchen table, his hair was the color of dark sand. The gray, long-sleeved T-shirt he'd bought in Texarkana stretched taut across his wide shoulders and deep chest. Her gaze roamed up his strong corded neck, the blunt planes of his face, the smooth firm lips she could still feel against hers. That she wanted to feel in other places.

Her attention rested on his whiskered face. The four days' growth was more than she'd ever seen. The only times she'd seen him unshaven were when he'd gone on weeklong deer hunts with her brothers. The scruffy beard did nothing to soften his blunt features.

It did give him an unfamiliarity she found intriguing. As if he were a stranger inside a body she knew well. The contrast struck a chord deep inside her, kindling a dark, new temptation.

It made her wonder what things she didn't know about him.

Remembering the soft scrape of his beard against her chin when he'd kissed her, heat flushed her body. "What is your life like now?"

He looked up, his face guarded.

"Can you tell me anything? Should I not ask?"

"I can tell you some." He sat back, laying down his pen and easing his chair a few inches away from the table. "What do you want to know?"

"Do you have a different name?"

"The first name is Greg. I shouldn't tell you the last name."

She tilted her head. "I can't see you as a Greg."

"You're not the only one," he said drily. "Sometimes,

I still don't realize people are talking to me when they call me that. It's weird. I want to tell them my real name."

"That has to be hard." And it sounded agonizingly lonely. "You said you work as a car mechanic. Are you a volunteer fireman?"

"No. If you're in the Witness Security Program, it's best to keep away from any aspect of your former life. Or that's what they say," he added bitterly.

"You can have friends, though, right? You don't have to stay away from society, do you?"

"No, not at all. I have friends. My neighbor Ralph and I play poker one night a week. He's not as good as Aaron, but he's beat me plenty."

She caught the wistfulness in his words. "Do you socialize with anyone from work?"

"Not really. I get along with all of them, but don't feel comfortable just hanging out."

"Ever spend time with women?" The question was out before she could stop it.

His gaze measured her. "No."

She couldn't imagine that he'd been celibate since their breakup and she wanted to ask if he'd been with anyone. On second thought, she didn't want to know.

"Most nights, I work on trying to figure out the mystery ingredient in the disappearing accelerant." A grin hitched up one corner of his mouth. "Have you learned how to cook? Or do you eat out all the time?"

"Hey, I cook a little!"

"Pouring cereal in a bowl isn't cooking, Meredith."

She laughed at his dry remark. "Okay, I usually pick

up something and eat at home, unless Terra or Robin take pity on me and invite me over for a meal."

She remembered all the times he'd cooked for her. Especially his wonderful breakfasts in bed after she'd worked a wretchedly long shift. It would be better not to bring that up.

She gestured toward his face. "Are you planning to grow a beard?"

"No. I just can't shave—I mean, I haven't shaved yet."

Maybe he wasn't strong enough yet to shave on his own? Or his shoulder hurt too badly? "Do you need help? I could help you."

"No." The word was flat, hard and his face closed against her.

"I don't mind."

"No touching, remember?" He didn't snarl the words, but close.

Meredith's spine went to steel and she sat up straighter. So, last night *had* affected him.

His gaze fixed on her mouth, so long that she felt her body start to soften.

Flustered by his focus, frustrated by how badly she wanted him, she spoke without thinking, "We've done fine when I check your wound. That involves touching."

A muscle in his jaw flexed. "Not the same thing, not by a long shot."

"It wouldn't take very long. Think how good it would feel to shave it off."

"No."

"Oh, good grief, Gage! I didn't say we would do it naked."

His eyes went dark, savagely hot as he said in a harsh voice, "You touch me, I'm touching you."

She blinked.

"How much of that do you think I can stand?" He stood, his chair scraping across the tile floor. "Hell, I couldn't even close my eyes last night. All I could do was feel you."

"You're the one who wanted to share body heat," she muttered.

He gave her a scathing look. Her heart hammered hard.

He jerked his thumb toward the bedroom which they had to pass through to get to its adjoining bath. "If you're up for it, baby, let's go. Give me a green light. I've waited a long time to get my hands on you again."

Oh, wow. She couldn't breathe. The heavy-lidded look he gave her burned right through her clothes. Had he always been this intense?

He was aroused. So was she. But she also sensed pain beneath his words.

She rose, palms slick with sweat. "I'm sorry. You're right. I should've realized, but... I'm sorry."

She couldn't tell if it was disappointment or anger that had his jaw firming. She wanted to touch him. Wanted him to touch her. Talk about walking right into stupid.

"I think I'll get ready for bed." Her voice shook.

"I'll sleep out here on the couch."

"We should take shifts, keep watch."

He grunted.

Feeling hollow, she walked around the sofa, heading down the hall. "Let me know when it's my turn. You need to rest, too."

He didn't say anything. A glance over her shoulder showed him sitting back down. Instead of immediately opening his notebook, Gage closed his eyes and pinched the bridge of his nose. Tension vibrated in his body.

Last night had affected him as much as it had her. It didn't give her any satisfaction to learn he'd been as wound up over it as she had. Instead, she felt sad.

She shut the bedroom door, her heart aching.

All day, she'd wanted to touch him. She still did. She told herself to dismiss it, to stop thinking about that kiss, but she couldn't stop thinking about it.

Because she wanted him, too. And that was the worst thing for both of them.

She was killing him. Being this close to her was going to snarl his guts into a permanent kink, especially now that he'd finally had another taste of her. Gage wanted to hit something. Even now, hours later, he could *still* taste her. And one kiss wasn't going to be enough.

Thanks to Meredith being plastered to him like cling wrap last night, Gage had been hard and hurting for hours. It wasn't until they got to the cabin that he had finally managed to get a little relief. Then she'd asked questions about his other life and started in on the shaving thing. That had fired him up again and brought back the feel of her lush curves against his back, the dark sweetness of her mouth.

Arousal had mixed with anger, started a slow boil inside him. Which was why he had told her point-blank what she could expect if she touched him. She couldn't just change the rules whenever she felt like it. If she couldn't make up her mind about what she wanted, he'd do it for her. Because he knew exactly what he wanted. Her.

She may have finally gone to bed, but her scent still lingered. Even so, that was easier to deal with than her sitting in the living area looking at him with those liquid blue eyes.

He bit back a groan. He'd nearly tumbled her onto that couch and kissed her until she agreed to do anything he wanted.

His resistance to her was *thisclose* to finished. Despite the smallness of the cabin, he planned to keep as much physical distance between them as possible.

He hadn't been able to gather his thoughts while she moved around. Went back and forth. *Breathed.*

With his concentration split like that, it would've been easy to miss something helpful in his notes so he started at the beginning. It took him fifteen minutes to settle down and focus his attention.

After a few hours, a headache throbbed behind his eyes. He rose from his chair at the table and walked to the narrow window left of the front door. Bracing his good shoulder against the wall, he stared out into the night, over the shallow porch, the red packed-earth road, the trees beyond. The moon was a cold sliver of ice in an inky sky.

"Is everything okay?" Meredith asked.

He started, his head whipping toward her.

"Sorry. I tried not to come up on your right, but your other side was against the wall."

He wished he hadn't told her about his loss of peripheral vision, but with her training there was no way to get around it. She was barefoot, which explained why he hadn't heard her. Her hair was down and she wore her pink leopard-print pajama bottoms and the pink long-sleeved cotton top that snugged her breasts just right. In two seconds, he could slip right under her shirt and have his hands on her.

He directed his gaze back out the window. "Everything's fine. Why?"

"I saw the light on. Is it my turn to take a shift?"

"No, go on back to bed. I'll do it tonight."

"But you said you didn't get any sleep last night."

He sure as hell didn't need her to remind him. "I took a nap this afternoon. Plus I want to go over my notes again."

"Any luck figuring out your mystery accelerant?"

"Not yet." Even the smell of recently brewed coffee didn't mask her light frothy scent. He straightened, cursing softly. "The answer's probably right under my nose, an ingredient or a combination I haven't considered."

She came closer, close enough that if he reached out, he could stroke her silky skin. Jamming his hands in his jeans pockets, Gage clenched his jaw tight.

"Would it help to talk it out? I know a little chemistry."

Talking wasn't what he needed help with. He needed to get her out of pouncing distance. "I don't know."

"I might see something you didn't."

Her chemistry background would be helpful, but he'd only just gotten his body past their earlier conversation. As he dragged his gaze over her, he wanted to move in closer, kiss her, peel off her clothes. Especially when he saw her nipples tighten under his perusal.

She realized where he was looking and backed up a step, a delicate blush playing over her cheeks. Seeing her brother's denim shirt on the back of the chair where Gage had hung it, she grabbed it and slipped it on. Folding her arms, she met his gaze defiantly.

It didn't matter that she was warning him off. If possible, his body wound even tighter. Accepting her help would force him to share more space with her than he wanted, but he needed a fresh pair of eyes. And if he tried anything, she would knock him into next week. "All right, yeah."

Her blue eyes widened. "Oh. Okay, good."

He moved around her, trying to ignore her provocative body-warmed scent. She followed him, taking the chair next to his and scooting closer.

Hell. She'd told him she wasn't interested. That should've been enough to cool him off, but it wasn't. He pushed his notebook to her and while she began reading, he recounted his progress.

"So far, I've determined the accelerant is an egg-based gelled flame fuel."

She looked up, frowning. "Gelled, like jelly?"

"Right."

"Not a liquid."

He shook his head. "If it were, there would be a trail of accelerant. Even concrete can soak up liquids and none of the surfaces in these blazes—concrete, wood or fabric—have retained anything. The fire-starting material has to be something that doesn't penetrate."

"And a jellylike substance wouldn't?"

"It normally would, but it could be coated to prevent that from happening."

"Coated? With wax?"

"Probably."

"So, the flammable gel is made of eggs—"

"Egg whites."

"Okay. Egg whites and gasoline then thickened with—" She glanced down. "Salt and tea leaves?"

"Those are only two possibilities. Further in the notes, you can see I also tested cocoa, sugar, baking soda, Epsom salts." He leaned over her to flip the page and point to the details he'd noted.

His muscles clenched against the teasing drift of her breath against his cheek. When she bent her head to read, her hair brushed the back of his hand.

He pulled away.

"A lot of things can work as a thickener, but I'm trying to determine if more thickener is the secret to making the accelerant disappear or if it's a specific ingredient."

"That's why it's taking so long to find an answer."

"Yeah."

As she went back to reading, he eased away, his attention fully engaged by her even though he wasn't looking at her. He was riding the edge of want. Was she?

After a few minutes, she looked up, her eyes crystal-blue in the light. She indicated a place in his notes. "I think you're right about the coating on the flammable jelly being wax. It would prevent a rapid breakdown, but wouldn't the wax also leave a trace?"

"Generally, but I think the reason it doesn't is because of what is mixed with it."

"And that's what we need to figure out."

He murmured agreement, forcing his gaze away from the pulse tapping in the hollow of her throat.

"So, egg whites, gasoline, thickener and wax. What kind of wax? Candle-making wax?"

"I tested that and also the wax used for preserving food, for canning. So far, that one seems to work the best."

"Isn't wax flammable?"

"Yeah."

"Which means if it's too hot when the gas-jelly is dipped in it, a fire could start if the temperature is misjudged by even a small bit."

He nodded. "That's why I think whoever is behind this is someone with extensive fire training."

"Or they're a chemist."

"That's possible, I guess." Gage had considered that in the beginning, but his gut said no.

She thumbed through a couple of pages. "You've tried granulated cane sugar. How about powdered sugar? Brown sugar? Or syrup?"

He grinned. "I like the way your mind works."

The slow smile she gave him had his heart knocking hard against his chest.

"Let's make a list of what I've tested and similar products I haven't," he suggested.

Meredith read aloud while he jotted down the possibilities. She was methodical and thorough, one of the few people who had ever matched him in that regard. They had always been able to help each other with problems in their jobs, but they hadn't ever done it while trying to ignore this fierce awareness between them.

He didn't know how long he could hold out.

Chapter 7

The next day, just before noon, Meredith stood at the front window of the cabin, her nerves jangling. Where was Gage? What was taking so long?

He had left a note saying he'd discovered a flat on the SUV this morning and had gone to get a new tire. The drive from here to the nearest gas station took about twenty minutes. So, there and back equaled less than an hour. Maybe another half-hour to pay for the tire and mount it himself. But he'd been gone nearly four hours.

What if that Julio guy had found Gage? Or what if Gage had seen the Hispanic man and tried to lose him by going back up into the mountains, then was unable to find his way down? He had a cell phone, she consoled herself. So, if something had happened, he would've called.

Unless he was hurt and couldn't.

What if Julio *had* hurt him and Gage disappeared? Just like a year ago.

The thought put a hard knot in Meredith's belly. What would she do if he didn't return? What *could* she do? Call his friend, the State Attorney General, and tell him.

Meredith wasn't typically a worrier, but from the moment Gage had shown up in her lake house, bleeding profusely, things had been unpredictable and weird to say the least.

The crunch of gravel and the soft rumble of a motor had her easing to the side of the window, out of view. A silver SUV passed by—Gage's vehicle—and she leaned into the wall, eyes stinging at her overwhelming relief. He was all right.

After a few seconds, the automobile's door slammed and she walked to the back of the cabin, making sure it was Gage who got out of the SUV. Quickly wiping her eyes, she opened the door as he walked across the frozen, pine-needled ground and took the two steps up to the deck carrying a small plastic bag. Clean sharp air swirled inside as he walked through the door.

Not wanting him to know how worried she'd been, she managed to keep her voice light. "Everything go all right?"

"Yeah." He frowned as he shut the back door with his foot, glancing at his watch. "I guess I was gone longer than I expected, but we can't risk not having a good tire when we need to leave."

She preceded him to the kitchen, where he placed the

bag on the counter next to the sink. "I bought a couple of cell phones—untrackable."

Not wanting to reveal how worked up she'd made herself, she kept her face averted.

"There was no trouble," he said. "I just wanted to make sure I wasn't followed. And I wasn't."

"That's good." She stared blankly at the plastic sack.

Behind her, he opened the refrigerator door and studied the contents inside.

"The tire shop at the gas station where I stopped wasn't open yet so I had to wait."

"I see."

He hesitated then peered around her shoulder to look at her. His breath grazed her temple. "You weren't worried, were you?"

"No."

After watching her for a few seconds, he reached for her hand, then pulled back. "You *were* worried. I'm sorry. I should've called."

She wanted to brush off his apology, say she was fine, but instead she said, "If you'd gotten into some kind of trouble, I wouldn't have known what to do. Or how to find you. Or who to ask for help."

He stilled, as if the possibility had only then occurred to him, too. "If something happens and I can't contact you, call Ken Ivory. I'll write down the number for you."

"Okay."

He jammed his hands into the front pockets of his jeans. "Were you afraid I'd disappear? Again?"

That was exactly what she'd feared. She looked at

him then, her pulse skipping when she saw the concern in his blue eyes. After a moment, she nodded.

"I really am sorry." His gaze stroked over her, making her skin heat.

At that moment, Meredith really wanted to touch him. She caught herself and stepped away, giving a brittle laugh. "I'm fine. You know how I think everything to death. I just got carried away."

"Meredith—"

"You're here now and no one followed you," she said brightly. "That's what matters."

He studied her for a minute. "Wanna eat before we set up our lab?"

She nodded, taking his now-empty bag and folding it to place under the sink with the others. "I thought I'd call Terra."

His gaze sliced to her. "What? Why?"

"To ask for some chemistry help. I won't mention anything about you or the task force or any kind of trouble. If she asks, I'll tell her I can't explain why I need to know."

He was silent for a moment. "Use one of the new phones and keep it short. I don't think anyone's on to us, but the fewer chances we take, the better."

She agreed, calling her fire-investigator friend while Gage made grilled cheese sandwiches.

When she hung up and turned off the phone, he glanced at her. "Was she any help?"

"Maybe. I'll know when we start experimenting."

After a quick lunch and cleanup, they began. Meredith wished she hadn't been so transparent about her worry, but she couldn't just push aside her concern. Just as she hadn't been able to block the want that had started a slow throb in her blood last night when he'd warned her what would happen if she touched him.

That macho stuff usually aggravated her, but last night, for some perverse reason, she'd liked it. Enough that she'd dreamed about him. *Them.* Sweaty, hard-pulsing sex dreams that left her aching even now.

In an effort to cool her blood, she reminded herself how things ended between them eighteen months ago. Though she wanted him, she didn't want everything that came with wanting him.

But had she been the one to draw the line? Oh, no. It had been Gage.

After being stifled for so many months, her hormones were tap-dancing. She could tell herself it was because she hadn't been with anyone since him, but she knew her body wouldn't respond this way to just any man. It was Gage. He'd always affected her this way.

But Meredith wouldn't let herself get distracted by that. Or by brushing elbows with him. The glancing touches, the occasional graze of his hip against hers made her edgy, restless. Hungry. She didn't want to get involved with him again. Their problem was too fundamental—she'd always been second to his job—and he hadn't ever seemed willing to change. Meredith didn't know if a person *could* change that much. Or even if they should. Such single-minded focus was what made him excel at his job.

They stood shoulder to shoulder over the kitchen

counter. He smelled of the sharp outdoor air and woods and an earthy musk. She didn't know if their working so closely was such a good idea, but she wanted to help, so here they were.

They'd decided to test three thickeners at a time. That would enable them to keep track of their results without getting too much information at once.

To begin, they made the egg-based gasoline gel by separating the egg whites from the yolks, then pouring the whites into a jar and adding the fuel.

They chose powdered sugar, baking soda and Epsom salts as their first thickening agents. After adding those ingredients to the jars, Gage handed Meredith a cooking thermometer. "While I'm stirring the mixture, you heat up some water. Let me know when it's at sixty-five degrees."

"What are we doing?" She searched under the cabinet next to the store and pulled out a two-quart-sized saucepan.

"Making the gel thicker. After it cools to room temperature, we'll dip it in the paraffin."

They worked in silence for a bit and Meredith found her attention wandering to Gage. He worked with confident, yet careful movements. The smothering odor of gasoline grew stronger and she wrinkled her nose.

"Where are we going to set fire to this stuff?" she asked.

"Out back in the galvanized tub I found against the side of the cabin. We can fill some small buckets with water to have close by in case we accidentally torch something."

She nodded, watching as he delicately handled an

egg. She remembered his strong broad hands on her, touching her face, stroking the small of her back, trailing low across her stomach.

A sharp tug of desire jerked her to attention and she shifted away. Tension coiled in her shoulders. The cabin was starting to feel about as big as a cracker box.

She focused on the water heating on the stove. As she checked its temperature, she felt Gage's gaze do a slow glide down her body and back up. Even pretending to ignore him didn't stop the sparks of heat shooting through her whole body.

She wanted him just as much as he wanted her, maybe more considering she hadn't had sex since they'd split up. Had he? She wasn't asking.

He had loved her. Meredith had never doubted that, which made it more difficult to understand his unwillingness to get married. It had taken her months to realize and accept that he really didn't want to have a wedding, but once she had, she'd returned his ring.

She'd been willing to commit. He hadn't. Why?

She'd never known for sure. At the time, she'd been too hurt and angry to ask him. Did it matter why? Did it matter *now?*

Yes, she decided. She turned, resting her hip against the corner of the stove so she could see him. Water bubbled in the heating pot. A foot away, Gage stirred the contents of a jar, his spoon clinking against the glass.

In the quiet of the small kitchen, her words were stark, bald. "Why didn't you ever want to get married?"

He froze, spoon in midair over another jar, his back

to her. After a long moment, he laid the silverware on a paper towel and turned to face her. Both hands curled over the counter's edge, as if he were bracing himself.

"I did want to get married." His blue eyes burned into hers. "That's why I proposed."

If you'd wanted to get married, we would have! Meredith bit back the scathing words. "You wouldn't ever agree on a date or suggest one that worked for you."

He looked down at the floor, his jaw working. Then he seemed to come to a decision and lifted his gaze to hers. "I had this stupid idea that I'd be giving up more than I wanted to."

"More what?" She stiffened. "Freedom?"

"That, and control."

Stung, she couldn't breathe for a moment. "You make it sound like I was forcing you to get married. As if I could. You *were* the one who asked. When you propose to someone, it's supposed to be because you want to be with them, not because you feel like you can't get away from them."

"Don't put words in my mouth."

"Did I make you feel trapped?" Her voice thickened. "Chained to me?"

"No."

"Then what?"

"I never wanted to get away from you. I just wasn't ready for marriage, but I didn't know that until I went into WitSec. That's when I figured out my priorities weren't in good order. My priorities about a lot of things, not just us. But being away from…" He hesitated, making her wonder if he had started to say something else. "Being alone sorted them out pretty quickly. That's when I realized the things I'd been forced to give up, the things I'd been worried about giving up were the things I wanted the most."

"Gave up?" Blinking away tears, she couldn't keep the bitterness out of her voice. "Some of it you pushed away."

"I know, and I take responsibility for that. Losing you made me open my eyes."

"Oh, please."

"It's true, Meredith," he said fiercely.

Fiercely enough that she shivered. She softened. "It's better that you knew before we got married. I wish *I'd* known sooner."

"Why? So you could've broken up with me earlier?"

"No." His scornful tone tripped her anger, her hurt. "So I wouldn't have been disappointed over and over."

"Do you want me to apologize again?" His voice was rough with emotion. "Say what an idiot I was? Open up a vein?"

"No, I don't want anything like that."

"What, then?"

She thought he winced before he glanced away. The regret in his face was every bit as sharp as what she felt over them. Over what she'd just said. She mentally chided herself. She didn't want to hurt him, didn't want to hurt herself anymore. "It didn't work out and now I know why. I've always wondered. Thanks for telling me."

Right now she wanted to touch him more than anything. Those gas fumes must be going to her head. "I just wanted some answers."

"For closure?" he asked tiredly.

Meredith was afraid there would never be closure. She shook her head. "No, just answers."

He searched her eyes and it took supreme self-control to hide what was happening inside her. Finally, he nodded and turned back to stir the gas-gel mixture.

She felt as if she were going to shatter into tiny pieces. How could she stand so close to him and pretend she was over him? She didn't know, but somehow she would. He might've been the one to draw the line in their relationship, but she'd be the one to make sure they didn't cross it.

Damn it, she drove him crazy. Gage didn't see how he could be more conscious of her than he had been before the "marriage" talk, but he was.

As they worked together in the following hours, they kept their conversation strictly to the experiments or the news. But it was as if every second brought a heightened awareness of her, even outdoors.

The next afternoon, they stood on the small deck of the cabin, setting fire to another block of gasoline gel. The sun was bright, the air crisp. Images of Meredith, sharp and clear, and without the dark winter coat that hit her midthigh, looped through his brain.

He pictured the soft curve of her neck, the elegant line of her back, those long sleek legs and perfect backside. And even though the bite of gasoline drowned her subtle scent, Gage knew he could find it in the warm crook of her neck or at her wrist.

It was killing him.

Her question from yesterday still circled through his head. He hadn't wanted to tell her why he'd dragged his feet about getting married. Women never understood stuff like that exactly as men meant it, but he'd spent the past year letting her believe a lie. He wasn't lying to her about anything else.

He'd been crazy in love with her, so it had taken him a while to figure out why he hadn't wanted to set a date for their wedding. Now that he knew the reason, he didn't mind if Meredith knew, too. If he ever got a second chance with her—and he wasn't holding his breath—he wanted her to know he realized how wrong he'd been.

But explaining his reasons had put more distance between them. Gage told himself that was good because it was what she wanted. But it bugged the hell out of him.

Since yesterday, they'd tested and made detailed notes on nineteen combinations of accelerants. Each of the burned blocks of gel fuel had left residue from at least one of its ingredients, except for the last two. Only a trace remained of those so Gage wanted to test the same combinations using different amounts of certain elements and see what happened.

They were discussing which to try first when they were interrupted by a ring tone from inside the enclosed back porch. "Don't Stop Believin'" by Journey pegged the ringing phone as Meredith's. Setting Gage's notebook on the window ledge, she moved to answer it, the screened door clattering shut behind her.

With a cheerful greeting, she went inside the cabin. He wondered who was on the other end of the phone.

Four days. That was all he had left with her, depending on the outcome of the trial. And he had to keep his hands off her.

When she didn't return after a few minutes, Gage decided now was a good time for a break. They had yet to mix up the next gel sample so he gathered the tub and three small empty containers they'd used, then placed them just inside the screen door.

As he stepped into the welcome warmth of the cabin, he slipped off the down-lined coat Meredith had pestered him to buy in Texarkana. When he walked past the bedroom, he heard the low cadence of her voice. He hoped she didn't talk much longer. Just because they hadn't run up against any problems since their last cell phone call didn't mean their communications were safe.

He filled a tea kettle with water and set it on the stove to heat. After a couple of minutes, he heard her say goodbye to the caller and come down the short hallway toward the kitchen.

She stopped at the breakfast bar, looking across the counter where he stood next to the stove, dumping packets of cocoa mix into two mugs.

Before he could ask, she said, "That was Robin."

A call from Meredith's cop friend didn't automatically mean something was wrong, but the worry in her voice said there was. Gage's shoulders tightened. "Is your family all right?"

"Yes."

Relief rolled through him. When she didn't say anything more, he cocked his head. Her brow was furrowed and he could practically hear the wheels turning in her head. What was going on?

Sober-faced, she walked to the sofa and sat. Gage switched off the stove, moved the kettle of water to the hot pad on the counter and went to the matching red leather chair.

His knee brushed hers as he sank down into the seat. "What is it?"

The slow way she answered told him she was trying to remain calm. Concern shadowed her blue eyes. "Robin said someone broke into my house."

"What?" He stiffened in alarm.

"She's been going by my place to pick up my mail and check the house. When she went today, she discovered someone had been there. Nothing was taken that she could tell. They must have been interrupted."

Maybe, Gage thought, apprehension drumming through him.

"That isn't all. Early this morning, she had to stop by Presley Medical Center to take a statement. A nurse there told her a man with an Hispanic accent has called the hospital twice, wanting to speak to me, but when the nurse asked some questions, he hung up. Robin thinks that might've been the prowler's way of seeing if I was home."

After a minute, she said what Gage was thinking. "If the caller was Julio, he could've easily found out where I live *and* work from the dead marshal."

Julio also might've broken in to leave something, rather than take. The thought had Gage's nerves stretching taut.

"Robin's waiting to hear if any of the fingerprints found at the house are in the system."

Identifying prints would be a huge help. Gage hoped some were found. He had never gotten any prints from the Smoke Screen arsons because the torch had been careful not to leave any. Possibly because the arsonist knew that, despite popular belief, fingerprints didn't disappear in a fire. Which was another indicator that whoever was behind the arson ring had extensive fire knowledge. If the go-between who had set the Smoke Screen fires was the person who'd broken into Meredith's house, Detective Daly likely wouldn't get any prints, either.

"Terra told Robin about my call for some chemistry help."

The mention of Meredith's friend drew Gage's attention back to her.

"That plus the break-in and the fact that I've stayed down here longer than expected made her hinky. I told her everything was fine."

Her voice shook slightly and Gage checked the urge to take her hand. "That's good."

"That's why we haven't seen Julio." Meredith stood, her voice rising. "He's in Presley. There are pictures of Robin, Terra and me all over my house. What if he hurts them because he can't find me?"

"Let's not jump the gun." Gage got to his feet. "He probably can't identify them."

"If he's been watching my house, he'll recognize Robin from going there." Meredith sounded close to frantic as she paced to the opposite end of the couch. "And if she starts digging around, she could put herself in danger."

"She's a cop. She's good at protecting herself."

Meredith didn't look reassured. "I didn't breathe a word to either of them about you being alive or what we were doing, but Julio doesn't know that. He could think I told them."

It was true, which meant her friends might be in danger. Meredith definitely was, since the SOB was still looking for her.

Tension pulsed from her. Clasping her hands together tight enough to show white at the knuckles, she moved to the fireplace. "I need to warn them and my family."

"You can't." He reached for her, then pulled back. He hated this. He felt as if he'd be violating some sacred oath if he touched her in any way.

The flush of anger on her features didn't hide the fear also lurking there. "It's one thing for me to be involved in this, but them? What if my mom or dad go by the house? What if he hurts them?"

Gage understood her rising panic. It was bad enough when she worried about herself, but the idea that people she loved might be hurt stripped away her cool doctor persona. The same fierce loyalty and protectiveness had made her help Gage long after she should have stopped. "I'll call Ken Ivory and tell him what's happened."

"What can he do?"

"If it will make you feel better, I'll ask about having someone watch Terra and Robin. He won't be able to tell them about it, though."

"This is all because of you," she cried out, her eyes welling with tears.

It was, and the ripping, gouging hurt joined the guilt and regret he carried all the time. If he'd had any stones at all, he would've climbed right back into his SUV after she'd patched him up the first time, dragged himself out of her lake house on his belly if necessary. But he hadn't, and now here they were.

"I'm sorry, Meredith."

"I've got to call my family."

"We don't know what we're dealing with. Whoever broke in may have done nothing. Or he could've put a camera or microphones in your house."

Horror widened her eyes and she moved to the other side of the coffee table. "Robin won't know to look for anything. I need to tell her."

"You can't. Since nothing is missing, she'll try to figure out why someone broke in. She'll look at every inch of your house."

Gage cursed himself all over again for putting her in danger, but he couldn't let her warn her family. The risks to them *and* to Meredith would be even greater. If Julio thought her family might know about her killing the marshal or Gage coming back from the dead or the real mastermind behind those arsons, all hell would break loose.

Visibly trying to remain in control, she took a deep breath. "Can you call Ken now? Will you tell him about Robin and Terra, too?"

"Yes." The fear in her eyes hollowed out his gut. He wanted to go to her, put his arms around her, but he didn't. "If something were to happen, if Julio tries to threaten them, they can both take care of themselves.

Terra's husband is a cop. Robin is a cop. When I call Ken, I'll give him the addresses of your brothers and parents, too. He'll do something to help."

"Robin did say she planned to call Jack and tell him about the break-in and the phone calls to the hospital."

"That's good." Although Robin talking to Terra's husband didn't seem to reassure Meredith much. The rare vulnerability in her eyes had Gage's hands drawing up into fists so he wouldn't touch her. "Spencer will know what precautions to take and how to protect Terra."

"What if it's not enough?"

He had no answer. When he shook his head, a tear spilled down her cheek.

Gage couldn't help it. He went to her.

She edged away, around the corner of the sofa and he felt her withdrawal like a slap. "I need to be alone."

"Okay, yeah." Frustration and resentment rose at her obvious attempt to stay away from him.

She started down the hall.

"I'll bring you some hot chocolate—"

"No, thanks."

He ground his teeth. "If you need anything, I'll be on the deck."

She didn't respond, just went into the bedroom and shut the door.

He dragged a hand down his face. He wanted to go after her and just hold her, but it would be a mistake. Because if he got his hands on her again, he wasn't letting go.

Chapter 8

A few hours later, Meredith froze at the corner of the breakfast bar, her apology stuck in her throat. The round table was set with red earthenware plates, napkins, silverware and wineglasses. A toasty-lemony scent drifted to her. In the background, the Righteous Brothers crooned "You've Lost That Loving Feeling."

Gage looked up from the salad he was making. "Ready for supper?"

"What is this?" Her gaze skipped around the kitchen, over the two saucepans on the stove putting off a savory aroma, then back to the place settings. "What have you done?"

"Cooked?" With a crooked grin, he stepped over to the table and set down the bowl of mixed greens.

After what she'd said earlier, Meredith couldn't

believe he was even talking to her, let alone cooking. "I was awful to you earlier. Why would you do this?"

His gaze softened on her face before he turned away. "We have to eat, right?"

Her heart swelled painfully. He moved again to the table, carrying a bottle of chilled white wine and filling the two glasses.

"Have a seat." Returning with their plates, he placed them on the counter then opened the oven. The citrusy aroma of lemon-baked fish filled the small space.

She'd been planning to apologize even before this thoughtful gesture. "I'm sorry for what I said before, about this all being because of you."

"It *is,* Meredith."

"You have no more control over this than I do." Her nerves were raw from their close proximity, the waiting, being chased, hiding out, all of it. And the new fear that Julio could harm one of her best friends or family members had everything crashing in on her. "I was afraid and frustrated. You tried to reassure me and I jumped down your throat. I shouldn't have spoken to you that way."

"It's okay. You're entitled." Using a spatula, he slid one piece of fish from the baking pan onto a plate. "You were upset when you heard about the break-in at your house. I didn't like it, either. The situation is scary. You shouldn't even be involved in this."

"You wouldn't have put me in this position if you'd had a choice." She exchanged the filled plate for the empty one. "Will you accept my apology?"

"It isn't necessary, but okay."

She smiled, then noticed his smooth jawline. "You shaved."

"Yes."

The tautness of his voice tweaked at the tension that had been between them before she'd disappeared into the bedroom.

Changing the subject, she moved toward the table. "It smells wonderful."

He grinned and motioned her into a chair. "Stop stalling and find out for yourself."

They sat and Meredith bit into a flaky, tender piece of cod. "Oh, this is good!"

He took a bite, then gave a satisfied nod.

"You can't tell me you were getting tired of my specialty, sandwiches and soup."

"Just thought it would be nice to have something different."

"And wine. Wine is an excellent idea." Meredith studied him for a moment. While she'd been stewing, he'd been doing things, nice things.

In the background, Elvis began to sing "It's Now or Never." The overhead light glinted off the red plates. For a bit, the only sound, apart from the music, was the scrape of their silverware as they ate.

Gage glanced over. "I spoke to Ivory. He's going to have some people watch Robin and Terra. Your family, too."

"Thank you." The strong relief she felt had her wanting to grip his hand. Instead, she sipped at her wine, enjoying its crisp flavor.

As they ate, Gage asked about the man who had

been chief of the Oklahoma City Fire Department at the time of Gage's "demise" and Meredith updated him on current department politics.

She was still concerned about what might happen to her friends and family, but was reassured to know the State Attorney General was helping. She might've attributed her increasing calm to that, but when Gage made her laugh about something, she realized it was more due to him.

The atmosphere between them was comfortable as he told her he hadn't made any further progress with his tests that afternoon. They discussed everything from movies to music, and she began to relax.

He didn't act as if he were angry about her accusation earlier and Meredith was glad. Still, she noticed he was careful not to touch her. Not when she handed him her wineglass for a refill or when he passed her more steamed vegetables or reached for the salt. It drove her nuts.

Especially since she'd been thinking about what might have happened if she'd gone with him to the bedroom as he'd challenged a couple of days ago.

When they finished eating, he refused to let her help with cleanup. He poured her another glass of wine and sent her into the living room where he'd already turned on the gas fire. As she settled on the floor and rested back against the brick hearth, she snagged a magazine from a rack beside the television. Considering the way she'd acted earlier, she had expected coolness from Gage, not thoughtfulness. Her heart turned over in her chest.

The magazine was open, but her attention was on the big man in the kitchen. A faint lemony scent still hung in the air. He moved efficiently from the table to the sink, his shoulder looking stiff even though he didn't appear to be bothered by any pain there. Or by any of his other injuries.

The startling realization of how close he'd come to dying put a hard knot in her chest, just as it had when he'd told her that night on the mountain. The danger, the uncertainty weighed on her. It had to weigh on him, too.

Not wanting to put a damper on their evening, she turned her thoughts to dinner. When they'd been a couple, he had cooked for her frequently. He'd always said being a fireman gave him an edge over her because of the years he was responsible for meals on a regular basis at the firehouse. He was good at cooking, as he was at most things.

As he had been with her in the beginning.

From their first date, they had enjoyed each other's company without a single awkward, getting-to-know-you moment. And despite what had happened to them, being with him now steadied her. Even in these circumstances.

It also unlocked memories. The past was a dangerous place to visit and she'd tried desperately not to do it in the past eighteen months. She doubted Gage had intended for their supper to remind her of the way things used to be between them, but it did.

Without his wineglass, he joined her at the fireplace, easing down beside her. Bending one knee, he draped an arm over it. His other hand rested on his thigh.

"How's your shoulder?"

He glanced at it. "Not too bad."

"The stitches should be checked again tomorrow."

He nodded, reaching toward the coffee table for the television remote.

There was a good foot of space between them. Meredith should be glad for the distance; instead she was irritated. At him and herself. The less contact they had, the more she wanted.

When she'd come into the kitchen for supper, she'd been determined not to cross the line he'd drawn between them, but his thoughtfulness chipped away at her resolve.

"Remember the first time you cooked for me?" she asked. "It was breakfast." *In bed.* "You picked me up after a long shift and took me to your place."

"I remember." The way his voice deepened gave her a shiver.

After eating, they'd showered. And stayed in bed all day. A quick glance at his hot blue eyes told her he remembered everything as well as she did.

When an image of his hard naked body flashed through her mind, heat burned her neck and she looked away. "Thanks again for supper."

"You're welcome."

"You made me feel better. You always could." She was surprised at the sudden tears that stung her eyes.

Gage tilted his head back, staring at the ceiling. Her gaze trailed down the strong corded line of his neck. She wanted to trace it with her tongue, follow it to the hollow of his throat.

She sipped at her wine. He'd told her what would happen if she touched him. "You cooked for me, too, after the presentation I gave to the American Medical Association on burn treatment. That was the night—"

She stopped herself from reminding them both of the night she had realized she was in love with him.

They'd been dating about three months and that evening had been easy and quiet, much like tonight. Well, minus the danger and all the lies about his being dead.

"That's one of my favorite memories," she said.

"Mine, too," he murmured.

Sensation rippled through her, her smile faltering as she became aware of the words the Righteous Brothers sang. "Unchained Melody." Beside her, Gage stilled and she wondered if he was having the same memory that suddenly rushed over her.

A month after realizing her feelings for him, they'd come to her family's lake house. This song had been playing in the background the night he proposed on the back porch swing.

Suddenly, all the old feelings surged back. The deep joy they'd found in being together, the certainty that there was no one else for them, the belief they'd be together forever.

As she set her wineglass on the hearth, she looked over, her gaze locking with his. Yes, he remembered. His dark, half-lidded gaze made her body vibrate clear down to her toes.

Maybe it was the song—*their* song—but as the Righteous Brothers' smoky voices wrapped around her,

Meredith was swept into the past. All the good memories. She had missed him. She was tired of being without him. Before she even realized she'd moved, she leaned in and brushed her lips against his.

Gage froze, squashing the urge to haul her to him and crush his mouth to hers. After learning about the break-in at her house, he had seen how rattled she'd been. He'd wanted to do something nice for her, so he'd cooked. He hadn't expected *this* in return.

When he didn't move away, she kissed him again, a real kiss this time. Her soft lips coaxed his, teased, her tongue tickling the corner of his mouth before he let her in.

She tasted cool, honey-sweet. He wanted to strip her bare and drink her up. He wanted her to touch him. All over. All night.

By some unbelievable force of will, he managed to keep his hands to himself. Fierce need swelled inside him as he pulled back slightly. "Do you remember what I told you?"

Her gaze never left his. "Yes."

"Say it," he demanded roughly. Muscles coiling, he waited.

Waited to see exactly what she wanted, how far she would go. He saw a flicker of indecision and for one second he thought she would back off.

Then she whispered, "If I touch you, you touch me."

Hell, yes. He barely registered pulling her across his lap then taking her to the floor. Wasn't aware that he'd unbuttoned her soft plaid shirt until he pulled his mouth from hers to rake his teeth down her throat and found his fingers already curved around her breast.

He flicked the front clasp on her black lace bra. She spilled into his hand, soft and warm and perfect. His thumb rasped across her tight nipple.

She shifted beneath him, squeezing his thigh tight between hers and pushing her hands under his sweat-shirt to stroke his bare back. The broken way his name spilled from her throat jacked his pulse into overdrive.

Drawing in a deep breath of her faint apricot scent, Gage sank into a haze of sensation. He pushed aside the open edges of her shirt and looked at his sun-darkened skin against her creamy, petal-smooth flesh, flushed from his touch. He stroked his hand between her breasts then cupped her fullness. When he closed his mouth over her, she inhaled sharply. Chest tightening, his blood hammered in his veins.

The whole time he'd been in WitSec, he remem-bered being with her—how she felt beneath him, the way her breath caught when he slid inside her, the way she always linked hands with him afterward, as if she thought he might leave.

Murmuring, she pulled his head back to hers and kissed him. The hand on her breast trembled slightly. Beneath his touch, he felt her pulse jump.

He'd missed her like hell. He had no idea what was going on. All he knew was that she lay beneath him and he'd been waiting a damn long time to get her there.

One of her soft, hot hands dipped below the waist of his jeans, scoring the small of his back with her nails. Burning need spiked inside him. She slid the other palm around his waist to his stomach. A second later, his jeans were open and her hand moved inside his boxers.

She curled her fingers around him. The sigh she made against his mouth nearly set him off.

Some part of his brain still worked. Searching for control, he lifted his head, his breathing labored. Firelight chased across her rose-and-cream features. Dreamy blue eyes stared up into his.

"You sure about this?"

"Yes." Slipping one hand out from under his sweatshirt, she skimmed her fingers down his clean-shaven jaw. "I want you."

Wild blond curls fell across one cheek and part of her eye. He nudged them away, grazing his thumb across her cheekbone. She was so beautiful, it hurt to look at her.

His gaze tracked down her body and Meredith's heart nearly pounded out of her chest.

He slid her shirt off. She pressed against him, her lace and satin bra open so nothing was between their hot skin.

He kissed her until she couldn't feel her legs, drawing the strength from her before trailing his lips down her neck. Sliding one arm beneath her, he supported her as he laved and nipped his way to the swell of her breasts. He tugged off her bra, curling his tongue around her rosy puckered flesh.

"Oh, wow." She twisted against him. "Gage."

He opened her jeans, slipped his hand into her panties and curled his fingers inside her. A ragged moan spilled out of her throat.

The feel of his slightly rough flesh against the smoothness of hers had heat flashing across Meredith's skin and she thrust her hands into his hair, trying to steady herself. His every touch was slow and thorough. She'd always loved that, but she couldn't handle it this time.

That intensity focused on her was thrilling. And terrifying. She didn't want to feel everything she'd always felt with him. The emotion was too raw, tapped too much of the pain from their past. She needed him to hurry.

Shoving up his sweatshirt, she flexed her hands in the wiry golden hair on his chest. He was hot and solid.

Reaching behind him, he pulled his shirt over his head and dropped it. She rolled him to his back, careful of his injured shoulder. He filled his hands with her breasts and lifted up to take one nipple in his mouth.

Her throat went tight. "Let me touch you, Gage."

He allowed her to slide down his body. His fingers skimmed over her back, her shoulders, as she kissed his neck, breathing in the scent of man and soap. She slid her lips to his chest, scraped her teeth over his nipples, kept moving.

A sound rumbled out of him. He was breathing hard, one hand cupping her head. "Slow down, baby."

"No." A low throb worked through her body and she was taken aback by a sudden sting of tears.

She wrestled his jeans and boxers past his muscled thighs. Following the garments down his body, she nipped his flat stomach just below his navel then moved lower to do it again.

"Son of a—" He pulled her up, fastening his mouth on hers.

Worked every time, Meredith thought as he rolled her to her back. He slid his big hands into her panties and pushed them off.

"Hurry," she breathed against his mouth. She wriggled, wanting—needing—him to move now.

Holding her head, he settled between her thighs. His hot straining flesh pushed against her. Meredith wanted to look away from the raw desire blazing in his eyes, but she couldn't move. She could barely breathe.

She tightened her legs around his hips and he pressed against her.

Then froze. "Damn it!"

"What?" she cried out, her short nails digging into biceps of pure steel.

He straightened his arms, bracing himself over her. Color burned across his cheekbones. He was breathing hard, his arousal throbbing against her inner thigh. "I don't have protection. I haven't been with anyone since you so I haven't needed anything—"

"You were my last, too." She urged him closer. "Don't stop!"

Eyes glittering with savage desire, his jaw worked as he stared down at their bodies.

The intensity on his face made her shiver. "I'm still on the pill. We're both cle— Oh!"

He thrust hard, his arms going under her and pulling her tight into his chest.

As she buried her face in his neck, emotions swamped her. Old, new, good and bad. As right as

Gage felt inside her, against her, her heart ached. She couldn't bear it.

He began to move and her vision hazed at the sharp tight contractions that started almost immediately.

"No, baby, hold on." Taken aback by her quick climax, he could barely get the words out. He fought to control his body. "This is too fast."

"It's good." Breathing in his heady male musk, she pulled his earlobe between her teeth.

He hissed in a breath, fisting a hand in her hair and bringing her head up so he could crush his mouth to hers.

She shifted, her body meeting his at a higher angle. He moved deep and sure, driving into her until she came apart beneath him, then he went, too.

As their pulses slowed, her hands stroked the supple length of his spine.

He nuzzled her neck. His voice was thick, gritty. "Damn."

"Yeah." Both her voice and body shook. She tried desperately to keep from letting him back into her head, her heart. She told herself to get up, say good-night, but she couldn't move. Didn't want to.

Nor did she want to allow the thought that had gnawed at her since she'd jumped him, but it pushed through, anyway. She had more than crossed the line he'd drawn. She'd plowed right over it.

And she hoped she wouldn't come to regret it.

A few hours later, Gage woke in the king-size bed where they'd moved after making love in front of the fireplace. The empty space next to him registered about the same time he saw Meredith at the window, wrapped in a blanket. Bright moonlight washed through the half-open blinds, tinting her profile with silver, gilding her hair.

Was she all right? She'd acted fine after they'd made love, had been the one to lead him to the bedroom. Now she stood perfectly still staring out the window.

Gage slid out of bed, ignoring the chill as he padded over to stand behind her. He cupped her shoulders, pulling her back against him and murmuring into her hair, "You okay?"

"Yes." She snuggled against him. "It's snowing. I was watching."

He slid his arms around her waist and pressed a kiss to her temple. "Pretty, and I'm not talking about the snow."

He felt her smile. "Aren't you cold?"

"You could warm me up."

She slipped off the blanket and he wrapped it around both of them. For a few minutes, they watched the snow swirl and dip in the frosty light.

Holding Meredith like this—naked and warm against him—wound him up tight. Of course, it didn't take much. He wanted her again. The first time had been great, but too fast. It had been about quenching a need, about taking. The whole time he'd half expected her to pull away, but he kept going. He'd wanted her for so long he wasn't going to let anything stop them.

They were surrounded by the quiet fall of snow, the stillness outside and in, the bare hum of the heater. He pressed tight against her bottom. When she pressed back, he nuzzled her neck. Lifting her left arm, he anchored it behind his head, opening her body to him, causing the blanket to sag off his shoulders.

She held his free arm to her stomach, catching their covering. Gage trailed his fingers down the underside of her arm, coasted them lightly against the curve of her breast to her waist.

A giggle escaped her as she jerked against him. "That tickles!"

He grinned and turned her to face him, her soft breasts teasing the hair on his chest. In the pearly light, her eyes glittered with dark desire. Keeping the blanket around them, he lightly grazed his mouth over her cheekbone, her lips, the line of her jaw.

Her eyes closed and the pleasure spreading across her face had him moving in for a kiss. Long and deep and slow. He knew she liked it that way. He tried to throttle back and give it to her as he feathered his thumb across her taut velvety nipple.

Both her hands flattened against his chest. He could stand here all night kissing her, but when he felt her shiver from the cold, he scooped her up and carried her to bed. As he followed her down, she tossed away the blanket and scooted close as he pulled the comforter and sheet over them.

Her kiss was fierce, demanding, but he wasn't going to be rushed this time. Rolling her to her back, he moved between her legs, linking his fingers with hers to bring their arms slightly above her head.

He dragged his mouth to her ear, down her neck. At the feel of his tongue there, she melted into him, shifting with him, using the length of her body to stroke him every time he touched her.

His lips glided down her throat and she bent her knees to give him more room. He took his time, teasing heated, openmouthed kisses all over her breasts, low across her belly, the inside of her thighs. By the time he put his mouth on her, she was trembling, his name a breathy plea that had him sliding inside her.

He struggled to still the urgency, pausing when her eyes fluttered shut. "Look at me, baby," he commanded raggedly.

She did and Gage thought he caught a flicker of wariness in the blue depths. He stroked her hair and moved slowly, even when she locked her legs around his hips and tried to speed him up. As she neared climax, he backed off.

A broken moan rose from her. He could feel the heat beneath her skin, the pumping of her heart against his. Kissing her deeply, he took her up again and again. Long minutes later, when the demanding pulses of her body sent him hurtling toward the edge, he nudged her over. She let go and so did he.

His spine felt like mush. He rested his head beside hers, soaking in her sweet fragrance, not wanting to move. Finally, he propped himself up on one elbow and brushed her hair off her face. "I've missed you."

She smiled, but it didn't reach her eyes.

He rolled to the side, taking her with him. His pulse slowed and she settled close. She was unlocking places inside him, stirring up something he hadn't felt in over a year—hope. Being with her felt familiar, but now he appreciated even more what he'd gone without for the past eighteen months. Maybe that was what made him finally realize she was holding back. She had the first time, too.

At first, anger swirled inside him. She was the one who'd initiated the sex, not him. But after their broken engagement, the way he'd hurt her, why wouldn't she be guarded?

Maybe she needed to know he wanted a lot more than this. He pulled her half on top of him, stroking his hand up and down the velvet of her back.

"Mmm," she breathed into his chest.

He brushed a kiss against her hair. "You can count on me, Meredith. I'm in this all the way."

She stilled, her fingers plucking at the hair on his chest. "In what?"

"This. Us. I want more of you than in bed."

She lifted her head, looking dazed. "What?"

"I want you back. I want things like they were before."

Unease suddenly pulsed from her. "What we're doing right now is nice."

Her wariness irritated him. "You saying you don't want more? Baby, you wouldn't have slept with me unless you were open to giving us another shot."

"I wanted you."

"You only wanted sex, nothing else?"

"Yes."

He snorted. "Bull."

She untangled herself from him and sat up, taking the sheet with her. Pushing her hair back out of her face, she turned toward him. "Gage—"

"So you won't even talk about giving us another chance?"

Her pale silky breasts swelled over the top of the sheet. Unable to resist the tempting fullness, he traced a finger into her cleavage.

She drew the sheet tighter around her. "After the trial, I may never see you again."

"Yes, you will," he growled, pulling his hand away from her soft flesh to push up on his elbows. "And that's not an answer. If everything at the trial worked out so that I didn't have to go back into witness protection, if I came back to my old life, my *real* life, would you give us another chance?"

"We don't know what will happen. Why are we even talking about this?"

"'Cause we just had sex. Twice. And it meant something to me."

When she looked away without responding, his gut hollowed out. What was going on with her? He sat up, turned her face to his. "I never forgot how things were with us."

"Not forgetting is very different from going back."

"It's a start." He trailed his thumb down her neck, grazing the delicate line of her collarbone. "Neither of us has moved on. That's significant."

"I don't know what you want me to say."

"I want you to tell me you want more than this."

"We have right now. That's enough."

Since when? Who was this woman? "You can't expect me to believe sex is all you want."

"It doesn't matter what either of us wants." Her voice

was steady, almost flat. "Not until the trial's over, anyway. After that, you're probably going back into WitSec."

Her pragmatic statement irritated him even though she was probably right. She still felt something for him—he knew she did—but what exactly? He searched her face, his heart squeezing tight at the careful blankness there.

Gage wanted to push her for an answer, but he was afraid it would be no. Plus, he couldn't ignore the bleak and very real possibility he might have to disappear again.

"I want to be with you. You want to be with me, so what's the problem?" She let the sheet fall, placing a hand on his thigh.

He wanted to hit something, but maybe in the time they had left before the trial, he could convince her he was serious about a future with her. A future he wasn't going to screw up. As soon as possible, he would figure out how to make that happen.

He cupped her nape and pulled her to him. Angry that she wouldn't talk about their life after this, his kiss was hard at first. Until she climbed into his lap and straddled him, her breasts teasing his chest, her soft silky heat scattering his thoughts.

Sex was all she wanted to give him, and it was damn good. But it wasn't enough. Even now with their bodies locked together, an emptiness hollowed out his chest. He needed to prove she could trust him, which meant he had his work cut out for him.

He wanted all of her. And he was going to have her. Somehow.

Chapter 9

Gage had thought nothing could add to his frustration about Meredith and her refusal to consider anything with them beyond right now, but he was wrong.

Late the next afternoon, he rapped on the bathroom door. In response to Meredith's "Come in," he walked into a warm fragrant haze of woman smells.

"I figured it out." Gage paused, taking her in. She lay stretched out in the tub, her head resting against the rim. His gaze slid from her upswept hair to the elegant line of her neck and the damp sheen of her shoulders. What the water didn't cover of her breasts, the bubbles from the apricot-scented bath wash did. He thought about getting in there with her, even though he hadn't been invited. "I know what it is."

Her drowsy blue gaze met his. "You figured out the mystery ingredient?"

"Yeah." Remembering how she hated cool air interfering with her bath, Gage closed the door before she asked. Bracing his backside against the sink, he crossed his feet at the ankles.

He and Meredith had worked on the experiments together until about twenty minutes earlier, when she had announced that she would fix supper after taking a bath. Thick perfumed steam swirled around him, settled in his lungs. Man, her scent drove him crazy.

He paced the two steps to the opposite wall then back to the door. "And my big discovery isn't going to do us any good."

"What do you mean?" She shifted so that water covered her shoulders, rosy skin peeking through the light froth of bubbles. A few damp blond strands escaped from the messy topknot and stuck to her nape.

His blood was on slow simmer for her anyway and the frustrating discovery about the accelerant edged him into a full-blown burn. He wanted to grab her and…do stuff.

He tried not to look at her. "The mystery ingredient that enables the gas-gel to disappear is—get ready—powdered sugar."

"Powdered sugar?" Her surprise was as palpable as his own. "You're sure?"

"Yes." He shoved a hand through his hair. "I tested it five times. Every time, the accelerant disappeared without a trace."

His gaze touched on her delicate earlobe, the droplet of water in the hollow where her neck met her shoulder. Stopping at the swell of her breasts, he remembered the softness of her fine-grained skin. He wanted to feel it again.

Noticing where he looked, she sank down a little lower in the tub. "…Larry James?"

Realizing she was talking, Gage jerked his gaze to her face. "Sorry, what?"

"I asked if there was any way for you to tie the powdered sugar to Larry James?"

"No." Gage's body tightened in anticipation of her getting out. "I was really hoping the ingredient I isolated would be some sophisticated compound or specialty material like that used in fireproofing or by stunt people. If it had been one of those, I could've at least checked to see if James had a connection to any company or person with access to something like that, but it's just plain powdered sugar and paraffin wax."

"What is it about the powdered sugar that makes the accelerant disappear?"

"From what I can tell, it's the amount." He fought the urge to pound his fist through the wall. "Damn it, this is all I have."

"You'll find another way."

"I hope so," he muttered, realizing she was finished with her bath and had been for some time.

But she stayed in the water, her body hidden beneath the bubbles. Why didn't she get out? It wasn't as if he hadn't seen and touched every inch of her. "Want me to get you a towel?"

"Not yet."

She wouldn't look at him and Gage ground his teeth.

Did her guarded behavior mean she regretted last night? She hadn't pushed him away, but everything she did was marked by wariness.

What had he thought? he jeered. That one night with him would erase her doubts, make her as certain about him as he was about her?

He wanted to grab her and kiss her until she melted. And she would, he knew. But there was too much at stake. As frustrated as he was with her, Gage knew he had to let her work it out on her own. When they'd been engaged, he'd made it all about him. This time he couldn't do that. Not if he wanted to show her he'd really changed.

"Are you going to get that?" She arched a brow.

"What?"

"Your cell phone."

At her words, he realized it was ringing. Pulling the phone from his jeans pocket, he answered. "Yeah?"

"Parrish, it's Ivory."

Gage mouthed the Attorney General's name to Meredith.

As the other man spoke, tension coiled through Gage's body. He could feel Meredith's concerned gaze on him.

He disconnected and she sat up straighter in the tub. The water gave her skin the luster of a pearl. "What is it?"

"A body matching Julio's description was discovered, shot execution style." Gage knew Meredith had worked the E.R. long enough to know that meant a bullet or two to the head. "Ivory needs us to look at the body, see if it's the piece of scum who broke into your lake house and shot at us."

"And tailed us?"

He nodded, feeling as if his chest were being crushed.

"I'm sorry." She searched his eyes. "If it is Julio, you may have just lost your last chance to connect Larry James to the arson ring."

"Yeah. Ivory wants us to come to Presley to look at the body."

"Now?"

Gage nodded, biting back a curse.

Meredith looked into his face for a long moment and he wished he knew what she was thinking. He wasn't ready to end their time together. He was no closer to getting his life back than he had been before running into her at the lake house.

"Let me look at your stitches before we leave."

"Okay. I'll check around the cabin outside, make sure no one's waiting to ambush us." He didn't care how tentative she was. He was damn well touching her. Pushing away from the counter, he stepped over to the tub and ran the backs of his fingers down her cheek.

She didn't pull away, but didn't relax into his touch, either. "What happens when we get back? Are you going to check in with the Marshals Service?"

"No. Even if the dead man is Julio, we still don't know the identity or whereabouts of the mastermind behind the arson ring. I don't trust anyone but myself to keep you safe." He frowned, suddenly hit by a thought. "We need a place to stay. We can't go to your house and I don't even have one now."

"Do you need to be close to the courthouse in downtown Oklahoma City? Does it matter?"

"I'm more concerned about safety than proximity."

"We could probably stay at Robin's," Meredith ventured. "But we would have to tell her some of what's going on and you might not want to do that."

"Does she still live outside the city limits?"

"Yes, on the acreage she bought several years ago for her horses."

Gage thought for a moment. "That might be good. She's a cop. We know she can keep a secret. She can protect herself, if necessary. But as you said before, there's a chance Julio and the ringleader might have made a connection because she's been house-sitting for you. And no one would think to look for us there. Do you think she'd mind?"

"No, but I need to find out if it's even an option."

"Okay. Use the second throwaway phone I bought in Texarkana to call her, then turn it off. We've been testing our luck with the personal phones."

"All right."

He reached over to the bar on the wall and snagged a towel, holding it open for her.

After a hesitation that had his jaw clenching, she gave him a small smile. "I'm still not ready to get out."

Gage fought the urge to reach down and pull her wet, slippery body right out of there. She wasn't ready to get out. She wasn't ready to talk about giving them another chance. What the hell *was* she ready for? If it had to do with him, apparently not a damn thing.

The watchfulness in her blue eyes told him whatever she felt about last night hadn't settled a part of her the way it had him.

Did she regret sleeping with him? He sure as hell

wasn't asking, but why else would she act this way? He knew what they'd shared meant something to her. It wasn't like Meredith to sleep with him just to scratch an itch. Or at least it hadn't been her way before he'd hurt her, he reminded himself harshly.

She hadn't hinted that she was thinking about what he'd said last night, but he hoped she was. He had to figure out a way to convince her he was in it for the long haul this time.

If the body discovered by the Attorney General *was* Julio, Gage was glad the bastard had been eliminated as a threat, especially for Meredith's sake. But as she had pointed out, he could possibly have just lost his last connection to Larry James.

Gage had made no progress on the case or with Meredith. He hoped he hadn't lost his last chance with both of them.

He was getting to her. Meredith had known he would and she was prepared. Sort of. Though she was jittery, so far she had managed not to give in to the hope that things could be different for them.

The sex was as good as ever, although now there was an added poignancy. Every time he touched her, it was as if he thought it might be for the last time. And it might be. The closer the trial got, the stronger the possibility grew.

Because Gage's SUV could be recognized by the still-unidentified man who'd followed them in Broken Bow, they'd decided to leave it at the lake house, returning to Presley in Meredith's Thunderbird.

When Meredith had called to ask her friend for a place to stay, Robin had agreed immediately. She'd also said she knew something weird was going on and wanted Meredith to fill her in when she arrived. There was no way Robin would guess Gage was at the center of that something weird.

A sense of sadness had swept over Meredith when they left the Greens' cabin. She wasn't sure if it was because of the uncertainty about the upcoming trial or because she had realized how difficult it was going to be to walk away from Gage again.

While secluded with him, there had been no choice except to live in the moment. And Meredith thought she was handling it fine until late that night as they stood on the wide wraparound porch of Robin's century-old farmhouse. When her longtime friend answered Meredith's knock, doubt sizzled through her.

With her dark hair pulled up in a ponytail and wearing flannel pajamas, Robin Daly looked more like a teenager than a decorated detective. She opened the screen door and pulled Meredith into a hug. "I'm glad you made it without any problems. I was starting to wonder. Come on in."

"I didn't tell you everything."

The other woman laughed. "You can tell me inside. It's cold out here."

"I'm not alone."

Robin frowned, looked past Meredith's shoulder to the circular gravel drive beyond. "Okay."

Gage stepped silently out of the deep shadows to Robin's left and she spun toward the movement.

"Hey, Robin," he said quietly.

For two heartbeats, the petite brunette looked non-plussed, then her classic features slipped into a polite unreadable mask. Her cop face. "Gage Parrish? Wow."

Despite Robin's reputation for being practically un-flappable, Meredith was surprised at how quickly her friend regained her composure upon seeing a supposedly dead man. She was probably already sizing up the situation.

"Witness protection?" she asked evenly as she ush-ered them inside and closed the door.

Meredith exchanged a look with Gage as he con-firmed the other woman's guess. It was a good thing he'd already decided to tell Robin everything. His main concern was Meredith's safety and even if her friend was furious with him, he believed she would keep quiet for Meredith's protection.

Robin crossed the living room, the large area warmed by a fire burning in a gray stone fireplace. The space was updated with dark furniture, wood flooring and cheerful rugs in a deep red. Family portraits in antique frames, an old grandfather clock and a rocking chair in the corner integrated the old with the new. "Put your stuff down somewhere in here. Y'all want something to eat?"

"No, thanks." Meredith draped hers and Gage's coats over the back of a taupe ultrasuede sofa and followed their hostess into the kitchen.

"How about something to drink— Okay, I have to sit down. This is too wild." She plopped into a chair at the light oak dining table. "I *knew* something was hinky when I talked to you, but I never figured this."

Meredith had only seen her friend this rattled one other time and she wasn't sure what to make of it. "How did you put together so fast that he's been in the Witness Security Program?"

"His death was obviously faked and the trial for the arsonists he busted is coming up. Makes sense the prosecution would want to protect their witnesses. I guess none of the other task-force members are really dead, either."

"The last I heard, they weren't," he answered somberly as he pulled out a hard-backed dining chair for Meredith then eased down into the one next to her. "But that was a year ago. I don't know about now."

The same dark flooring carried over from the living area. The dining table was centered in the big room finished with dark blue counters and white cabinets. A large picture window gave the kitchen an airy, open feel. Meredith noticed her friend's holstered gun and badge on the nearest counter top.

She hadn't been sure how Robin would react to seeing Gage. The policewoman had always made clear that she thought he was a bonehead for letting Meredith get away.

Meredith glanced over at Gage. "This okay?"

"Sure, if it's okay with Robin."

A slight frown gathered on the other woman's brow as she looked at them both. "Of course, you can stay. Meredith, did you know about this? His being alive?"

"Not until several days ago."

"It was a big surprise to her, too." Gage linked his fingers with hers.

At his touch, Meredith stiffened, but didn't pull away. Nor did she respond when he gave her a sideways look. "That's an understatement. I nearly passed out when I saw him bleeding over the sink."

She related how Gage had believed the Borens lake house to be empty and had gone there for medical supplies.

"Gunshot wound," he offered. He described how he'd been shot by Marshal Nowlin, about how he and Meredith had been caught off guard when the marshal and an Hispanic man showed up at the lake house.

Robin's eyes widened as she looked at Meredith. "You shot the marshal?"

"Good thing she did or I'd be dead," Gage said. "She's saved my life twice."

Robin stared hard at Meredith. "Damn, girl."

"Tell me about it," she muttered.

Gage continued, "We plan to lay low until the trial."

"Which is supposed to start in two days," Robin said.

He nodded. "I called the Attorney General on our way up here. He wants us to identify the body of a man matching the description of the intruder who shot at us in Broken Bow. And we both have to be deposed about the marshal."

"You can stay here as long as you want."

The offer was sincere, but Meredith could see the frost slowly gathering in her friend's eyes and in her manner toward Gage. Robin hadn't completely forgiven him for the way he'd hurt Meredith.

"I've been working the break-in at your house," Robin said. "But haven't gotten anything new. Didn't find any prints, not even a smudge. Do you think it was this Julio guy?"

"Very probable," Gage said. "We never found any prints at the arson fires we think he started."

Meredith recognized the glint in her friend's blue eyes. Robin was about to burst with questions—for Meredith, not Gage.

He finally caught on, too, and stood. "I'm outta here so y'all can talk."

Their hostess indicated the hall on the other side of the living area. "There are two guest bedrooms. Take your pick."

"Thanks." Gage lightly squeezed Meredith's hand before starting into the living room.

"Be careful with your shoulder," she cautioned as he scooped up her bag along with his. She watched him go, feeling a mix of uncertainty and longing and regret.

Robin muttered something under her breath and pushed out of her chair. "Parrish?"

Meredith's gaze shifted from Gage to her friend on the other side of the table. Uh-oh. She had seen that give-me-a-reason-to-shoot-you look before.

Turning, Gage paused in the archway. "Yeah?"

"Because of what happened at my 'wedding that wasn't,' I've made it a point to stay out of other people's business."

His big frame tensed and he waited. At Robin's mention of being jilted at the altar, Meredith frowned. Her friend hardly ever talked about that horrible day anymore.

The brunette nailed Gage with a look. "But if you hurt Meredith again, that will become my business. Got it?"

"Robin!" Meredith exclaimed, but neither her friend nor Gage looked at her.

His eyes narrowed and Meredith could practically see sparks shooting off both of them. One second stretched into another. Even though Robin's gun was still on the counter, Meredith's heart began pounding hard. Robin started to stand.

"Got it," Gage said.

Startled by his response, Meredith drew in a breath. She felt surprise from Robin, too.

With a half grin, he raised one hand in the air as if surrendering and said in his best John Wayne imitation, "I don't want any trouble. I'm gonna walk out of here real slow, Detective."

It broke the tension and Meredith smiled. Robin's mouth curved slightly.

His gaze shifted to Meredith. "See you in a bit."

"Okay."

Robin remained standing until Gage disappeared from sight then she plunked down in her chair. "Good grief! Seeing him had to be a huge shock."

"It was."

"Are you okay?"

"I'm fine. The first couple of days weren't so good."

"I wish we could tell Terra about this," Robin said. "Just what all happened down there? Are y'all back together? What are you thinking?"

Meredith drew one foot under her. "Which question do you want me to answer first?"

The brunette made a face. "Well, I don't want to know *exactly* what all happened down there, but are y'all back together?"

"For now."

"For now," her friend repeated. "Not forever?"

Meredith shook her head. "Last time, I didn't know things between us would end. This time, I do."

This past week, she and Gage had come close to being killed. She *had* killed someone. If anything had been hammered home to her, it was that all you had was the moment.

"If the guy who shot at us and trailed us around the lake is dead, that means Gage has lost his last chance to find something incriminating to nail the mastermind behind the arson ring."

"So even if those on trial are convicted, his life will still be in danger and he'll have to disappear again."

"Yes."

"Meredith, this could really happen. Are you sure you want to let him that close?"

She started to say she'd gone into this with her eyes open, that she knew what she was doing, but she *didn't* know. The only thing she felt certain of was she couldn't handle more pain like that of last time. "I won't let him hurt me again."

"How can you help it? You're still in love with him," her friend asserted quietly.

The comment caused Meredith's stomach to fall to her feet, but she didn't deny it. "This isn't about love—it's about commitment. To each other first, then our jobs. He still has the drive, the single-minded focus he had before, but he seems to genuinely regret how things ended."

She explained how Gage had apologized, how he had taken responsibility for what had happened to break their engagement. "And he's been acting differently. More…thoughtful toward me."

"That could be because he hasn't seen you in a year and a half," Robin pointed out wryly.

Meredith nodded in painful agreement. "I've thought about that. Before, he didn't value our relationship enough to put me ahead of his job. What's to say he would give it any more priority than he ever did?"

Compassion and understanding darkened Robin's eyes. "I don't want him to break your heart a second time."

"It's not high on my list, either." The memory of last night swept over her. His tenderness, his refusal to make the sex as casual as she had wanted. His sincere desire to go back to the way things were. Her heart squeezed. "I've never felt this way about another man, but I don't trust him not to hurt me again."

"So, what about after the trial? What will you do if he doesn't have to go back into the program?"

"I don't know." She couldn't think in terms of the future. Gage might believe he could reclaim his life, but Meredith didn't. She couldn't afford to. "I just don't know."

Annoyed and impatient, Gage lay on the fluffy queen-size mattress in the bedroom closest to the kitchen.

He'd caught snatches of Meredith's conversation with her friend, enough to remind him how deeply he'd hurt her. As if he needed reminding.

He would never forget the raw pain in those blue eyes—pain he had caused—when she'd broken off their engagement and he wondered, not for the first time, if she could ever get past it.

The women's voices dropped to murmurs and he heard them say good-night. The kitchen went dark, leaving a lamp glowing from the living room to throw light into the hall.

He heard the soft scuff of shoes against the carpet, then Meredith paused in the doorway, blocking the light. For a long moment, she stood in silence outside the half-open door. Her hesitation to enter the room set off a burst of anger inside him. Damn it!

She still didn't trust him. He didn't blame her—she had plenty of reason not to. But, hell, what did he have to do?

She may have gotten naked with him last night, but she had been skittish ever since. When he'd taken her hand earlier, she'd gone as stiff as a tow bar.

Mounting frustration and deep regret snarled his gut into a knot. He knew he couldn't pressure her even though every cell in his body strained for her to come to him. So he waited. And hoped.

Chapter 10

Gage's irritation about the case and now Meredith edged into anger. If he clenched his jaw any tighter, he was bound to break some teeth. He was surprised enamel wasn't shooting out his ears. The next morning, he and Meredith drove south on Hefner Parkway from Robin's house.

He'd eagerly accepted her offer to let him drive the fiftieth-anniversary-edition car, but tension still vibrated between them as it had since they'd eaten, dressed and started this trip to the Oklahoma City morgue to identify the man suspected to be Julio.

Meredith's light, luscious scent taunted him as did the tousled blond curls she'd tamed into a neat twist. He wanted to sink his hands into her hair and mess it up, touch her petal-soft skin. But her blue eyes kept him from doing anything. They were distant, a reminder she wasn't his and might never be again. As if he needed a reminder after last night.

After long moments of standing outside the bedroom door last night, she'd finally come to bed. She had slept against him, but she hadn't really been there. Just like now.

She was with him, but not *with him.*

She wouldn't let him in past a certain point and he had no idea what to do about it. Force the issue? That would be suicide, but ignoring it bugged him, too.

She was the first to break the silence. "Maybe we'll learn something at the morgue."

"That would be nice," he said tightly.

"Do you have a plan for after this?"

He didn't know what the hell it would be. Do his part at the trial and hope someone else found something to incriminate Larry James so Gage could get his life back? "Not really."

"I'm sorry. I know how frustrating this is for you."

"That isn't the only thing frustrating me." He wasn't fazed by the sharp look she gave him. His discontent about their relationship—about *her*—was no secret.

She opened her mouth as if to say something, only to be interrupted by a burst of song from her cell phone. After a quick glance at the call screen, she looked at Gage in surprise. "It's my neighbor Sarah."

"It's okay to take it."

"All right." She answered, then grew eerily still. "Wait, slow down."

At the shock on her face, concern shot through him, then surprise as she reached for his hand.

Meredith held on tight, grateful Gage was with her. A buzzing had started in her ears at her neighbor's first words. She managed to reply to the other woman calmly, but her nerves wound tighter and tighter. After a few moments, she hung up, feeling ill and detached.

Gage squeezed her hand. "Baby?"

Reeling, she shook her head. "Sarah said there's been a fire at my house."

"What!"

"She saw the smoke and called 9-1-1. The fire department got there quickly and the fire's out now, but she doesn't know how much damage was done." Her voice thickened. "She said it's still standing. That's good. Maybe it isn't too bad."

He cursed under his breath as he changed lanes. Meredith was riding the edge of numbness and fear. She wanted to curse, too. Or scream at someone.

She still had a home, but how much of one? She felt completely lost, bereft. For an instant, on a lesser scale, she had an inkling of how alone and displaced Gage must've felt when he lost his home. His whole life.

She began to tremble. "I can't believe this."

"Are you okay?"

The worry that carved lines in his face had Meredith trying to shake off her dazed lethargy. "Yes."

She was amazed at how calm she sounded. She wasn't calm. She couldn't even make herself release her choke hold on his big hand.

It was a second before she realized he'd exited the parkway. "What are you doing?"

"You sure you're all right? You look pale."

"I'm okay." Her voice quavered.

Gage turned the car around and drove to the ramp going the opposite direction. Once again on the parkway, they traveled back the way they'd come.

Meredith frowned. "Where are you going?"

"To your house."

"But… What if someone sees us there?" Her grip tightened on his. She couldn't stop trembling.

"We'll stay a fair distance away."

"Are you sure this is a good idea?"

"We need to go there, baby."

"To check the damage? If it's risky for you, we shouldn't go."

"Partly to see the damage. We'll lay low, stay out of sight."

After struggling to steady her racing heartbeat, she nodded. Having Gage with her helped managed this adrenaline free-for-all.

With so many questions yet unanswered, she tried to figure out what might have happened. "It was probably an accident of some kind. Electrical. Sarah said she never saw anyone hanging around my place."

"Yeah, it could've been an accident." The cynical brusqueness of his tone told Meredith he didn't believe that. "That's one reason we need to check it out. We need to know exactly what we're dealing with."

Something in his voice had her considering another likelihood and her gaze locked in on him. "Do you think this is arson? Do you think it's related to your case?"

"I don't know, but I seriously doubt it's random.

Julio or whoever tried and *failed* to kill us is nowhere to be found, and now a fire is set at your house? You're still in danger. It can't be a coincidence."

The hair on her neck rose.

"I have to get inside and determine if the blaze was arson. I think it was, but I need to be sure."

Her hand felt cold in his. "How are you going to get in?"

"I don't know yet." He linked his strong, warm fingers with hers and Meredith held tight. "We'll figure it out."

Twenty minutes later, they pulled into her housing addition, able to get within only a block because of the police cruisers forming a border to keep people away from the fire scene. Red and blue lights strobed here and at the opposite end.

Parked on the next curb were two SUVs bearing the names and logos of Oklahoma City television stations. A helicopter belonging to another station circled overhead. Gage intended to stay under the radar.

He backed away from the cordoned-off area then parked on a side street half a block down. He and Meredith settled in to wait until the rescue personnel left her house. The acrid stench of smoke burned the cold air. The white-gray haze dissipating into the clouds told Gage the blaze hadn't been caused by petroleum products. Otherwise, the smoke would be dark.

Neither of them spoke. Waiting in the heavy silence, surrounded by Meredith's frothy scent, turned Gage's thoughts to them.

He was trying to give her the space and time she needed to make up her mind about them, to see he had changed, but it was gnawing a hole inside him. He told himself to be patient, just as he would be in an investigation. But he had trouble reining back when Meredith was concerned. Still, he had to try.

He couldn't do anything about his situation with her right now, but he could focus on this fire, determine if it was arson and find out if it was related to his case.

Finally, the police cruisers and fire trucks left the scene. As he and Meredith carefully made their way toward her house, midmorning sunlight speared ruthlessly into the shadowed corners of the established neighborhood. They stayed behind trees and kept an eye out for neighbors or anyone else they might see.

She had bought this house after she and Gage had gotten engaged, and though he had been inside plenty of times, they had split up before he could move in.

About a hundred yards from her cottage-style home, they stopped beside a gray brick house on the same side of the street as hers and Gage scanned her now-soggy front yard. Water from the fire hoses soaked the cold packed ground, streamed down the pavement and glistened on nearby trees. Yellow crime-scene tape stretched around the house and yard.

A policeman watched the scene from his patrol car at the curb.

After scanning the area again, Gage said in a half whisper, "I don't think Presley's fire investigators have shown up yet or they'd still be working inside. Since they aren't here, it means they're probably at another scene. A big one, if it required both Terra and Collier McClain to work it. That's good for us."

"What are we going to do? That cop is looking this way." Meredith kept her voice quiet. "It's not as if we can just stroll inside."

"I'll figure out something."

A few minutes later, they had a plan. Gage waited as Meredith returned for her car, then drove into the neighborhood as if just arriving. When she walked toward the patrol car, Gage took advantage of the officer's distraction and slipped over a chain-link fence behind the gray house and then another, moving toward Meredith's backyard through those of her neighbors.

He encountered a basset hound inside one fence, then a mastiff inside another. Both dogs began to bark. They continued to make noise as Gage kept moving and finally climbed over Meredith's taller wooden fence into her backyard. Though he couldn't hear her, he knew she was doing as they'd agreed by telling the patrolman the damaged house was hers and asking to be let inside.

Knowing the cop would refuse to allow her into a scene that hadn't been processed, Gage used the key she'd given him to let himself in the sliding glass doors at the back of her house.

He quietly closed the door and took in his surroundings, noting there was no odor of kerosene or gasoline. That, along with the absence of black smoke, told him another type of accelerant had been used.

The center of the house was the open living room. An attached dining room looked out the front and the kitchen, which looked to have sustained the most damage, was to his left. He relaxed slightly, knowing the kitchen wasn't visible from the front windows.

The smell of wet ash hung in the air. Meredith's light gray carpet was soaked, covered with soot. Grime streaked the white walls and boot prints clearly showed the path the firefighters had taken to douse the blaze. Among the many questions Gage wanted to ask was if they'd used the typical wide or "fog pattern" spray to kill the fire. But of course he couldn't ask.

Nor could he dig for answers since he was without his shovel. Even though he hadn't performed fire investigations for a year, his hand still felt empty without his most essential tool.

The firefighters had entered through the front door, moved into the charcoal-filmed living room then the kitchen. The room's cabinets, counters and floors were blackened. At the kitchen's back wall, the doorway that led to the laundry room was charred. The kitchen was the point of origin and the alligator-patterned frame was the low point, the specific place the fire had started.

Using Meredith's cell phone camera, Gage snapped pictures of the sooty foyer and living room before turning to the kitchen to search out more detail.

He started at the kitchen's back wall, his attention immediately snagged by a cloudy yellow blob of gel attached to the other side of the door frame. This was no electrical fire.

His heart rate kicked into high as he moved closer.

Bingo! Gage knew this signature. The gel block in front of him appeared to be exactly like those he'd made for his experiments. All the torch had to do was adhere the accelerant to where he wanted and light it. Just like what had been done to start the arson ring fires.

He was barely able to stop himself from calling out to Meredith. Thank goodness for her neighbor who had gotten the fire department here in time to prevent major damage to the house, especially the kitchen. And to keep the evidence from burning and disappearing.

A nice-sized chunk of gel remained, enough to test and maybe lead to the mastermind behind the arson ring. And hopefully prove that person was Larry James as Gage had suspected all along.

Since there was no dead body at this scene, the fire department wouldn't need to work with the police department, but seeing as how both a cop and Presley's lead fire investigator were close friends of Meredith's, Gage was pretty sure he could get information about anything discovered here.

This fire was definitely arson, likely connected to Operation Smoke Screen. And this time, he had evidence to prove it.

Meredith could feel frustration rolling off Gage in waves. An hour after leaving her house, they were driving away from the Oklahoma City morgue and back to Robin's farmhouse. The man they'd been asked to identify had indeed been the man who'd tried to kill them, the one Gage said was the go-between who'd set the fires for the mastermind of the arson ring.

Julio Garza. They had his whole name now, and that

was all they had. No connection to Larry James, nothing on Garza's body or in his effects to point to anyone. Disappointment was a sharp keening pain in Meredith's chest. Judging by the way Gage's jaw muscles bunched, he felt the same way.

She drove while he used her cell phone to call Robin and take more notes. As he told the detective what he'd discovered about the fire at Meredith's house, she regained her mental balance enough to sort through what had happened. She realized with a flutter of panic that the first thing she'd done upon hearing the news about her house was turn to Gage. It had been natural, but she couldn't let herself depend on him. For anything. It would only lead to hurt.

Forcing away thoughts about the two of them, she listened to his conversation with Robin.

"We're leaving the morgue. The scum we identified was the guy who tried to kill us in Broken Bow. Since he was lying on a slab at the time, I know he didn't set the fire at Meredith's."

He paused, listened, then continued, "He never left prints at any of his scenes, but whoever torched Meredith's house might have. As thorough an investigator as Terra is, I'm sure she checks everything for prints at her fire scenes."

After answering a couple of questions and asking Robin to call with any news, he disconnected. Even though his voice had been steady while on the phone, Meredith heard the strain beneath his words. Recognized the stress that made his shoulders rigid and cut deep lines around his eyes.

As far as evidence went, Julio was the end of the road for Gage unless Terra discovered something at Meredith's house. Chances were high Gage would have to return to the Witness Security Program, and the possibility left Meredith feeling empty, sad.

He stared out the window of her car as she drove north in the noon traffic. Glancing at her, he pinched the bridge of his nose. "Did I sound as desperate as I feel?"

Meredith's heart ached. "There has to be something else we can do, somewhere we can look."

"I don't know what it would be."

His voice was gritty with exhaustion, his features haggard. The strain of the past couple of weeks rode him hard. She hated this. She might not know what she wanted for them, but she knew she wanted Gage to get his life back, wanted his grandparents to get their grandson back. Right now, it didn't seem likely.

"Maybe you could go through my house again," she said. "Or give your test notes to Terra and see if she can find something you may have missed."

He was quiet for a long moment, then reached over and took her hand. "What I care about more than anything is that you're safe. I want that for you, no matter what happens with me after the trial."

Tears stung her eyes. His going back into Witness Security would be the worst thing for him and his grandparents. It had cost him enough. Why did the person doing the right thing have to pay the price?

"Robin's going to keep me in the loop." He dragged his free hand down his face. "She'll let me know as soon as she hears anything from Terra."

Meredith squeezed his hand. "That's all we can do for now?"

"Yes." And it pissed him off.

His gut told him he'd uncovered something key at her house and it grated that he had to sit around on his hands and wait on someone else to find out what it was. Terra Spencer was one of the best fire investigators he knew, but Gage wanted to be the one working that scene. It was *his* life on the line.

Between that frustration and the feeling Meredith was getting farther from him, he was ready to chew nails. It didn't help that his damn shoulder was aching worse than it had in the past few days.

His patience, already flimsy, only wore thinner as the hours passed. Hours spent between reviewing everything he'd found at Meredith's house and thinking about his woman. Was it his imagination or was she spending most of her time in whatever room he wasn't in?

Irritation, resentment, bubbled up until his insides felt on fire. When his mood didn't improve the next day, Gage went in search of more things to do. He entered the last of the results of his and Meredith's experiments on the marshal's laptop, then e-mailed the schematic he'd found to Ken Ivory.

The ache in his shoulder had him looking on the Internet for some range-of-motion exercises. Sitting on the end of the queen-size bed he and Meredith had been sharing, he was about five minutes into the first set when her voice came from the doorway, startling him.

"What are you doing? You know I should check your stitches before you do something like that."

"My shoulder feels fine." He rolled it to demonstrate.

Looking pale and concerned, she walked toward him. "Let me see."

He unbuttoned and slid off his dark green long-sleeved shirt then sat quietly as she examined his injury. He drew in the deep scent of woman and apricot.

"It's healed well. Well enough to take out the stitches." She moved to the corner of the room where she had put the medical supplies she'd brought and returned with a small pair of curved scissors.

As she carefully removed the stitches, he watched her face, the tiny line between her brows as she concentrated. Watery winter light streamed through the window. His skin pulled with the removal of each suture. When she finished, she ran a gentle hand across his scar.

He looked at it. A healthy pink and healing scar. "Thanks."

"You're welcome."

He wanted to pull her into his lap, but didn't. Normally, he would've touched her before she did him, yet for the past couple of days he'd felt as if he needed to wait for her to make the first move on everything. It bugged the hell out of him.

Things between them were fine as long as he didn't talk about anything other than what was in the moment. When he did, Meredith closed up.

When she lightly ran her fingers through his hair, he settled a hand low on her hip, looking up at her.

"Are you about to go stir-crazy?" She moved away

to dispose of the sutures in a wastebasket the same navy as the other accents in the bedroom.

He stood, pulling on his shirt and buttoning it. "Yeah. I'm trying to keep my mind occupied."

Before she could reply, her cell phone rang. She answered then handed it to Gage. "It's Robin."

He took the phone, tamping down restlessness and a demand for the detective to tell him what she'd learned.

"Terra was able to get a couple of sets of prints, even one from the accelerant, but they were smeared," Robin said. "No match points at all."

Damn! Gage felt as if a massive weight crushed his chest, cutting off his air. What the hell was he supposed to do? How was he supposed to walk away from his life again? From Meredith? Would he ever nail the master-mind behind the arson ring?

His brain was churning so hard he almost missed Robin's next words.

"But we got something better."

He froze. "What?"

As he listened, adrenaline shot through him. His gaze went to Meredith, who watched him closely.

Whatever she saw on his face had her moving closer.

Excitement mounting, he struggled to wait for all of Robin's information. He wanted to be sure he had everything right. He could hardly wait to get off the phone. When he did, he grinned and scooped Meredith into his arms.

Hooking an arm around his neck for balance, she ordered breathlessly, "Tell me!"

"Terra found DNA."

"DNA! From what?" The elation in her voice matched his. "Blood? Hair?"

"She managed to extract it from oil left behind by the fingerprints."

"I've read about that process. I didn't know our lab could do that now."

Gage nodded. "The best part is that the DNA matches Larry James."

"Oh, how wonderful!" She hugged him tight.

Saying the words out loud made it seem real. Gage could have the bastard locked up for years. He wouldn't have to stay in witness protection. None of the task-force members would.

He actually felt weak with disbelief. Sorting through a flood of emotion, he buried his face in Meredith's thick fragrant hair. Finally, *finally,* he could nail that son of a bitch. He was going to close this case.

His mind was so full it took him a second to register Meredith's question.

"How was Terra able to get his DNA to test against what she found at my house? Is he in custody?"

"No. Robin said she's trying to serve a warrant on him, but so far he can't be found. Terra was able to match his DNA because it was in the system."

"Why would it be in the system? Oh, wait, I remember. Like a lot of cities after 9/11, Oklahoma City and Presley began storing samples of blood from rescue workers, like firefighters. That way, if something happens and they can't be identified by sight, they can be identified by DNA."

"Right."

"James's DNA would still be in the system even though he was fired?"

Gage nodded. "The city can barely afford to pay people to enter all that data. They sure aren't going to pay them to take it out."

Satisfaction filled him. He finally had the bastard. It didn't feel real yet, but it was. "Robin also said they'd gotten a warrant to search his house and turned up a gun along with some records. She thinks the ballistics will match the bullet that killed Julio."

"Did she say anything about the records?"

"Only that her first glance revealed details about fires. She thinks I'll be able to tell if the information concerns the arson ring blazes."

"Oh, Gage, I'm so glad for you." Her eyes filled with tears as she hugged him tight. "Your grandparents will be overwhelmed."

"That isn't all." Keeping her close, he drew back to look at her. "I'll have my life back, baby. *We'll* have our lives back."

Her bright smile faded.

"This isn't over yet, but I can see the end of it." He stroked a hand over her hair. "I may have to go back into Witness Security for a while, until Larry James is apprehended, but once he is, I'm coming back for you. We can be together."

"Gage."

The low warning in her voice had dread piercing through his euphoria, but he wanted her to know he was serious about a future with her. He'd kept quiet since the night they'd first slept together, but he wasn't keeping quiet now. "I know you think you can't trust me, but you can."

"I can't…do it again." She stepped out of his arms. "I can't be with you."

Her words didn't surprise him. Tension over this had been bubbling from the moment he'd told her he wanted things to be the way they were before.

"I've tried to give you space, Meredith. To show you I mean it when I say I've changed."

"It's not your sincerity I doubt. It's your commitment to me—to *us*. That a relationship means more than your…dedication to your job."

She'd been about to call it his obsession, he realized. And she would've been right, back then. "After what happened, the way I was last year, it's understandable why you'd still think so, but—"

"Before I returned your ring, I spent so much time trying to figure out what was wrong with me." Her voice shook and he couldn't tell if it was from pain or anger. "But I wasn't the problem."

"No, you weren't. It was all me." His heart clenched that she'd ever thought the fault had lain with her. "My job meant too much to me."

"I didn't leave because you cared about your job. I left because that was *all* you cared about."

She walked to the other side of the bed and he felt every inch of distance like a blow.

"Watching our relationship die nearly wrecked me. For weeks after I broke our engagement, I was out of it. Once I had to leave a surgery because I didn't trust myself not to botch it. I'm not willing to go there again. I'm not strong enough to handle us falling apart a second time."

Hadn't she noticed any difference in him at all? He told himself to be patient. They could work this out. "I'm nuts about you, Meredith. And I know you still feel something for me."

"That wasn't enough before. Why would it be now?"

"Because now I know what I gave up. I'm willing to compromise, not expect you to do it all. I finally understand how badly I hurt you and I'm not going to break your heart again. Look at me. You can see I'm telling the truth."

Her eyes, full of anguish, searched his. "I believe you."

"Then why won't you say yes?"

"Right now, you don't have to give your attention to anyone or anything except me. But once you're settled back into your life, your *job,* that will change."

"Things aren't going to be the way they were before, baby. Whatever it takes, I'm not going to lose you again."

"Please don't say things like that. We're…over. We both need to move on."

Irritation streaked through him. "If that's what you want, then why did you sleep with me?"

"Because I wanted to be with you," she said quietly. "It doesn't mean I think we can work."

"Then what *does* it mean?"

"I… Goodbye, I guess."

The sorrow in her voice didn't stop anger from roaring through him. "Did you ever even consider giving me another shot?"

"I can't."

"You mean you won't."

She hesitated. "Yes, that's what I mean."

His gut twisted into knots. "Is that why you slept with me? Because you figured it would never go anywhere? Damn it, Meredith, I can't prove I've changed if you won't let me in!"

"This isn't easy for me, either, Gage. In some ways, we're very good together, but not when it comes to forever. Not when it comes to putting us as a priority."

"That's on me and I'm different now." He shoved a hand through his hair, fighting not to panic. It couldn't be over. "I don't know how many ways to say it."

"I can't let you hurt me like that again."

"How long do I have to pay for my mistakes?"

"This has nothing to do with punishing you." She wrapped her arms around her waist, her eyes troubled. "It has to do with protecting myself."

From him. "I get it, okay. I should probably do the same damn thing, but I want to work through this."

After a long moment thick with pain and regret, her gaze lasered into his. "How do I know things will be different?"

His heart thumped hard. Was she softening? Would she give him another chance? Hesitantly, he reached out. When she didn't shy away, he stroked her cheek. He fixed his gaze on hers.

"Because while I was gone, I woke up every day wanting you with me and I don't want to wake up that way for the rest of my life. I know what it's like to be without you," he murmured. "I don't want to ever feel like that again. I can't make you believe me. Or trust me. The only thing I know to do is stick around and show you."

He saw the uncertainty in her eyes, held his breath in hope she would agree, even reluctantly, to give him another chance.

Then he saw her decision and her words shot his wish all to hell. "Don't. This is hard enough for both of us already. It's not fair to you or me."

His chest felt like a wide gaping hole; his voice turned sharp. "Why are you completely closing the door? Because I can't make any guarantees about us? Neither can you."

"We just don't work. You know it, even if you won't admit it."

"In the past, maybe that was true. Not now."

She shook her head, her blue eyes dark and sad. "You can really just walk away?"

"I have to."

"Well, I can't. I won't."

"Don't make this any more painful for either of us." Her voice quavered and tears filled her eyes. "If you really do still care for me, let it go."

"That's exactly why I can't."

She moved past him, not even pausing at his words. As he watched her leave the room, desperation and near-panic choked him. Was she truly finished with them?

He didn't want to believe it was over, but he didn't see how he could believe anything else.

Chapter 11

A little before eight the next morning, Meredith, Gage and Robin were shown into an empty courtroom the Attorney General had found to use as a waiting room. Meredith and Robin would wait here while Gage gave his deposition to Ken Ivory. Per Ivory's instruction, the three of them had arrived before court convened at nine o'clock.

As Meredith watched Gage and the AG walk through a corner door leading to the jury deliberation room, she was one big throbbing nerve.

Gage would be deposed first about her killing Marshal Nowlin and then how the marshal had tried to kill Gage. When it was time for her deposition, she would trade places with him.

Once he was out of earshot, Robin turned to Meredith,

concern in her blue eyes. "Sheesh, I nearly got frostbite in the car on the way down here. What's going on with you two?"

Tears tightened her throat. After her talk with Gage, she'd spent last night in Robin's other guest bedroom. Meredith had seen hurt in his eyes the first time she'd broken up with him, but if memory served, it hadn't been as raw or bleak as what she'd seen yesterday.

She and Gage had ridden to the courthouse with Robin at his insistence. He wanted more than himself watching out for Meredith. They had talked little during the drive and when they had, it was about things concerning the trial.

Her heart ached. "Once all this is over, he wants to try again, but I said no."

"So, that's why he looked like he wanted to shoot someone. Are you doubting your decision?"

"No. I don't know." She didn't think she should second-guess herself, but it was difficult not to. "I feel like I made the decision I should have, but it's not the one I wanted. I really do believe he's changed, that he wants to make our relationship a priority, but I can't trust he'll stay that way."

"After he settles back in and goes to work, you mean?"

"Yes. All I can think about is how he became obsessed with his job and put it ahead of everything else, including me. I can't let him hurt me like that again."

Robin gave her a quick hug. "I'm sorry."

"Thanks." Meredith wiped at her teary eyes. "I'm so ready for this to be over."

The pain was sharp and deep. One of the first things she'd learned in med school was to detach emotionally from certain situations. She had to distance herself now, from Gage, or she wouldn't be able to make it through the trial. And she needed to be here for him one last time.

Robin and Terra had offered to attend court with her for moral support, and Meredith was so grateful for her friends. They'd been through a lot together.

Terra's divorce, losing her friend and mentor to a serial arsonist, marrying the sexy cop she'd met on the case. Robin being jilted at the altar and nearly being killed in a fire. Meredith's breakup with Gage and her subsequent belief that he was dead. And now as she walked away from him for the second time.

Maybe Gage was right and being with him had been her way of saying goodbye. She'd foolishly believed they could spend these last several days together and she wouldn't hurt when it was over, but her heart felt just as shattered this time as it had the last.

She glanced at Robin, who wore a smart-looking navy pantsuit. "How long do you think his deposition will take?"

"Hard to say." Though Robin wasn't on duty today, she wore her badge, gun and holster clipped to the waistband of her slacks.

"I'm going to make a trip to the ladies' room."

"Why don't you go to the one used by the jury? Even though no one has spotted James, it's better if you don't go out to the public restrooms. While you're gone, I'll call Terra and check on her ETA."

Meredith nodded as she walked past the jury box and through a door made from the same dark wood as the rest of that in the high-ceilinged room. The facilities were across from the deliberation room where Gage was being deposed.

After a quick trip, she started back to the courtroom. Startled by a noise behind her, she glanced over her shoulder and saw a dark-haired man easily more than six feet tall. He was replacing a vent cover high on the wall.

At first, she tagged him as a maintenance worker. She smiled, then looked again. There was something familiar about his sharp-edged cheekbones, the slitted, cunning gaze—Larry James!

She'd seen his picture on the television enough the past couple of days to be sure. Managing not to betray the fact she'd recognized him, she played it cool and kept walking. She'd tell Robin, then Gage—

Something hard slammed into the side of her head and she crumpled to the floor in a burst of pain before everything went black.

Gage rubbed his nape as he walked out of the room where he'd been deposed by Ken Ivory and into the courtroom where he expected to find Meredith and Robin waiting. The room was empty.

Outside the main door, he could hear the increasing din of voices in the eight-story building. The tap and click of shoes echoed on the polished marble floor.

Where were Meredith and Robin? If Meredith had gone into the deliberation room, he would've passed her. He knew neither woman would leave this area. Most likely, one or both of them had gone to the restroom.

Stepping into the jury box, he eased down into the nearest chair and closed his eyes. Meredith had made it clear she was in no mood to talk, but they needed to. He intended to. He just wasn't sure if he should leave her alone a few hours or try to talk to her now.

"Son?"

At the familiar masculine voice, Gage jumped to his feet and pivoted. "Gramps? Gran?"

Owen and Millie Parrish rushed toward him. He met them halfway.

The tall, white-haired man and petite woman with frosted hair swept him up in a tight embrace.

"It *is* you! Thank goodness!" His grandmother's voice was tremulous.

He pulled back slightly to look at the older couple. "What are you doing here? Did you come for the trial?"

"Mr. Ivory wanted us to come. We didn't know why until just now." Owen Parrish's voice cracked.

Gage's grandmother touched his face, her soft hands shaking. "I can't believe it. You're alive."

She burst into tears and grabbed him to her. His own eyes stung as he met his grandfather's gaze. Looking as if he were having trouble holding back tears, too, the older man put a hand on Gage's shoulder.

After a long minute, Millie stepped away. She kept touching Gage, on the face, on the arm.

His grandfather hugged him hard. "Mr. Ivory filled us in on what's happened the last year. How are you doing?"

"Have you been eating?" Gran asked. "You look thin. And you need a haircut."

Chuckling, he urged them each into a chair in the jury box before taking the seat between them.

He quickly caught them up on his life for the past year, including how Meredith had found him wounded at her family's lake house and probably saved his life.

A fresh set of tears started in his grandmother's eyes.

He hugged her again. "I'm fine, Gran. And thanks to the investigation at Meredith's house fire, there's evidence to put away the scum who masterminded the arson ring. That means I don't have to stay in the Witness Security Program."

"That's the best news we've had in a year," his grandfather declared.

Millie's blue gaze pinned Gage. "And what about Meredith? How were things between y'all while you were together? I know you still have feelings for her. Is there any chance—"

"She's said no. Twice."

"She can't forgive you for putting her second to your job?"

"I think she has, but she's afraid I'll make the same mistake. She doesn't trust me."

"You did let work take precedence over everything, Gage," his grandmother reminded softly.

"I know. And I regret it. Living in WitSec has taught me a hard lesson. I won't make a mistake like that again."

"And you've told Meredith this?" Owen asked.

Just as Gage was about to answer, the door leading

from the jury deliberation room jerked open. Robin looked quickly around the courtroom, her face chalk-white.

Dread hammering through him, he slowly got to his feet. "What is it?"

"Meredith went to the jury's restroom. When she didn't return after a few minutes, I went to check on her. She wasn't there. I looked in the offices for the clerk and bailiff, and the court reporter. Finally, I found one of her shoes down the hall, near the door leading to the stairs. There's no sign of her."

"It's James, that SOB." Gage knew it without a doubt. He started toward the petite detective.

His grandfather rose, too, his deep voice concerned. "What can we do? Where should we start looking?"

"The best thing would be for y'all to stay here." Robin glanced at Gage. "I need to tell Ivory."

"We'll cover more ground if we help," Owen pointed out.

Robin glanced at Gage, her expression saying she was leaving the decision in his hands.

He shook his head. "This guy's out to get me, Gramps. He won't care who he hurts. It will be better if we don't have to worry about y'all, too."

The older man started to protest, but Gran put a hand on his arm. "We don't want to make things more difficult. If there's something we can do from here, tell us."

"Okay, thanks."

"Parrish!" Ken Ivory appeared in the doorway behind Robin.

The Attorney General's face was tight with worry. "I've contacted security and the police department. A

SWAT team is being deployed right now. They'll be here shortly."

"We can't wait on them!" Why were they standing around here talking? Irritated, Gage shoved a hand through his hair. "We need to find her now. Whatever Larry James is planning, he'll do it and get out. He won't stay to play hide-and-seek."

"Security has covered all the exits," Ivory informed him. "And when the SWAT team arrives—"

"I'm not waiting on them. I can't." Gage started around the man and Robin, who both stood in front of the door leading to the deliberation room.

Robin snagged his elbow. "Hold on—"

"The longer we wait," he gritted out, "the better the chance he'll get her out of here. Or do something worse. He wants me and the other witnesses dead. He won't care if he kills anyone else in the process. It's my fault Meredith's involved in this. I won't stand here and do nothing."

"I'll go with you." The brunette turned to follow him, pulling her weapon and checking it.

As they started down the hall, Ivory called out, "Parrish, tell me where you're going so I'll know how to direct SWAT."

"James will be looking for a way to get out without being noticed by too many people."

"He'll take the stairs," Robin predicted as they started down the hall. "He could go to the third or fifth floors and take a walkway over to the county office building."

"Or he could go down to the concourse," Gage said.

The detective nodded. "That connects to a parking garage north of the courthouse."

"Got it!" Ivory was already dialing his cell phone.

When Gage and Robin reached the door to the stairwell, she volunteered to take the flight leading up. Gage headed down, panic squeezing his chest. He had to find Meredith. If anything happened to her—

He cut off the thought, putting himself on autopilot, pushing his feelings away so he could do what needed to be done.

Down one flight of stairs, he passed a door marked Storage. He paused, turning to look back. This room would make a perfect place to hide while people checked exits first. The heavy door groaned as he opened it.

Well-used chairs, discarded tables made two neat rows. Past the furniture, battered and sagging file cabinets formed a line of corners and shadows that would make it difficult to be found.

Gage reined in the urge to sprint to the other end of the room. The fluorescent bulbs didn't provide the best lighting, but that wasn't the reason he had to jog rather than run.

Due to his loss of peripheral vision, he was forced to move slower and look at everything head-on or risk missing something that might help find Meredith.

A couple of minutes later, he was giving thanks for that same handicap. If he hadn't needed to make allowance for it, he would've missed the tip of a black shoe peeking out from behind a shadow-draped file cabinet.

Not just any black shoe. A woman's shoe. Meredith's shoe.

Gage knew because he remembered everything about what she'd worn to court. She looked sleek and professional in a black herringbone suit, her blond curls drawn into a neat twist at her nape. Those high heels made her legs look even better than they normally did.

Keeping his gaze on the shoe, he stopped several feet away. "Meredith?"

"Gage!" She stumbled into view, pushed from behind by Larry James.

The bastard held her in front of him with one arm locked around her torso. He towered behind her, holding a cell phone.

Meredith was calm, pale, but Gage saw the fear in her eyes. And a streak of blood at her left temple. Rage tore through him. "Are you okay?"

She nodded.

His voice was hard, vibrating with anger. "What did you do to her, you son of a bitch?"

"Nothing nearly as bad as what I'm going to." The ex-fire investigator held up the cell phone and Gage knew what the man had planned.

He'd planted his gel blocks and intended to detonate them all at once. The courthouse had been crawling with security since last night, so it was possible James had chosen a location other than the ventilation system for his accelerant. There was no way of telling how many gel blocks the scumbag had placed.

Gage's mouth went dry. "Let her go, Larry. There's no reason to keep her."

"After I kill you, I'm going to need her to get out of here."

Alarm flared in Meredith's eyes, then anger. Gage forced himself to keep his gaze on the other man, trying to think of a way to get his hands on that cell phone without hurting Meredith.

"The police department and a SWAT team are on their way. You're not going to get very far."

"With her, I can get as far as I need to."

The man was so bitter over being terminated from his job, he was willing to take revenge against someone who had no part in it at all. "She's not involved in this. You've gotten your revenge against all the men who had anything to do with you losing your job. You set them up, used a middleman to offer them bribes, which they took. All of them are locked up."

"And I'm not joining them."

"I wouldn't count on that. You threatened the marshal to get him to kill me, but he died instead so you had to send your go-between, Julio Garza, after me."

"You can't prove any of that." The other man tightened his arm around Meredith until she winced.

Gage barely managed to keep from going for the bastard. "Is that why you killed Garza? Because he didn't kill me, either?"

"Who says I killed *anybody?*" James sneered.

"It may never be proven and you may not pay for that murder, but you're going down one way or another." He kept his voice level. "You left your DNA at the fire at Meredith's house."

The man laughed. "Bull!"

"Our lab extracted oil from a fingerprint off the gel

block and from the oil, they managed to collect enough DNA to test. The sample matched yours."

For the first time, Gage saw a flicker of uncertainty in the bastard's eyes.

He quickly sized up the situation. Meredith still clutched her purse tightly to her chest, her other arm locked against her side by the man holding her. How could Gage get her out of the way before Larry James ignited the whole place? Neither he nor Meredith had a weapon.

"Parrish, back off or I'm going to start pushing buttons."

No way in hell was he backing off. Mind racing, his gaze locked on Meredith. She stared intently at him, almost desperately, and he realized she was going to make a move.

Before he could warn her to wait, James said, "This is what's going to happen. Parrish, you're going to leave—"

Moving suddenly, Meredith dropped her purse and reached back, grabbing James's throat.

The man choked and twisted away from her. She jerked around, chopping at his windpipe with the knife-edge of her hand. Gage lunged for the bastard and the cell phone.

Air gurgled in the back of James's throat and his face went fire-red. Dropping the phone to make a grab for Meredith, he fell to his knees.

Gage snatched the phone and punched the off button.

Before he could breathe a sigh of relief, a loud thud had him wheeling around. Larry James lay unmoving at Meredith's feet. Her gaze met Gage's and all the color drained from her face.

She wobbled and he reached out, putting a steadying hand on her elbow. His jaw clenched as his gaze went to her blood-streaked temple. "What did he do to you?"

"Hit me with something."

"You okay?"

"Yes." The cut looked stark and darkly raw against her pale skin. "Are you?"

"I'm fine, except for my heart nearly stopping when I found out he had you." Gage moved to plant his knee between James's shoulder blades and reached for the scumbag's arms. "You're sure you're all right?"

She nodded, gingerly fingering the side of her head.

"That was too damn close." He frowned down at a still-motionless Larry James. "That was some move. Learn it in med school?"

"Self-defense class," she half whispered.

Her trembling voice made him want to hold her, but he knew better than to try right now. There was still clear distance between them. Rage pumping through him, he shook James, who still hadn't moved. "Get up, you bastard."

Gage thought it odd that the SOB hadn't stirred. He found out why when Meredith knelt next to him and pressed her fingers to James's neck.

"No pulse," she said quietly. "He's dead."

Chapter 12

Minutes later, they were surrounded by SWAT, several OCPD officers, Attorney General Ivory, Robin and Gage's grandparents.

Meredith wasn't sure how many times she repeated her story. Because she'd seen James actually planting the accelerant, he couldn't leave her unconscious or dead. The risk was too great that someone might find her body before the explosion and alert people, so he had taken her as a hostage. Thank goodness Gage had shown up when he had.

Sitting in a chair several yards from James's body, Meredith answered questions from the Attorney General as she watched the steady activity around the scene.

Ken Ivory closed the notebook he'd been using to

record her answers. "I still need to depose you about the marshal, but I can do it another time."

"Could we go ahead? I'd prefer to finish everything now."

The man's gray gaze measured her. "If the paramedic says you're okay, we'll go back to the room we used before. Until things wrap up here, no one will be using that courtroom."

"Thank you."

She watched Gage talking to his retired boss as well as the new fire chief, Bill Haynes. Several firefighters passed by, all pausing to slap Gage's back or shake his hand, disbelieving smiles on their faces.

Presenting the evidence found at Meredith's house and the past pattern of James's behavior at the arsonring fires, Gage had managed to secure a couple of fire stations on standby. If James had managed to detonate those gel blocks, the fire department would've had a good chance of dousing the blazes before anyone was hurt.

She told herself to stop watching him.

A lanky, dark-haired paramedic approached and knelt next to her chair. "I need to check you out, Dr. Boren."

She nodded, recognizing him as a firefighter-paramedic who often brought patients into the Presley E.R. "Are you working for Oklahoma City now?"

"No, just doing some training with their SWAT medic program."

"I'd forgotten Presley started a program like that. It's a good idea to take paramedics on police calls. You look familiar, but I'm afraid I can't remember your name."

"Walker McClain." He gently examined the cut at her temple. "A while back, you saved my sister-in-law, Kiley, after she was shot."

"Oh, yes, you're Collier's brother." Something else about him nagged at her, but Meredith couldn't call it to mind. "Terra Spencer, the fire investigator who works with him, is one of my closest friends."

He nodded, moving in front of her to check her pupils. The hollowness in his eyes tugged at a memory. She felt as if she had treated him or someone with him at one time.

She knew she was focusing her attention on him rather than Gage because watching her ex was too difficult.

Then she remembered. Two years ago, she'd treated Walker McClain's pregnant wife after she'd been beaten. Sadly, neither the woman nor the baby had lived. Her heart clenched.

He cleaned the wound on Meredith's temple. "You don't need stitches. I can just put a butterfly bandage on this."

"Okay, thanks." She gave up trying not to look at Gage.

This might be one of the last times she saw him. She swallowed past a lump in her throat, admiring his big frame, the hard muscular line of his body. Seeing him with his former co-workers filled her with a bittersweet certainty. He was back where he belonged.

Walker's green gaze followed hers to where Gage stood with his former boss and his grandparents. "My brother's mentioned Parrish a few times. He's a good fire investigator."

"Yes, he is," she murmured. "He's outstanding."

And she couldn't take that away from him. She wouldn't. She'd been right before. Their lives just didn't mesh. Neither of them should have to change the core of who they were in order to make their relationship work.

Walker grinned. "Just before I got to you, I heard the new chief offer him his job back."

"That was fast." A razor-sharp pain lodged in her chest. She looked away, fixing her attention on the floor. "They'd be lucky to have him."

Walker finished bandaging her cut. "Okay, you're all set."

"Thanks." She rose, her attention again shifting to Gage.

The current fire chief approached Gage and after a minute, drew him aside. The two men talked intensely, then shook hands. Gage was taking the position. And why shouldn't he? Meredith asked herself. He no longer had to feel torn between his job and her. Before long, he would be immersed in another case.

Tearing her gaze from him, she found Robin and Terra waiting several feet away and joined them. As she walked away to give her deposition, she fought the urge to turn around and look at Gage one last time.

Ending things for good between them had been the right thing to do. And she didn't know if she'd ever get over it.

* * *

A few hours later, Meredith angrily dashed away a tear as she walked into the guest bedroom at Robin's. Her mind was filled with images of Gage, memories. Regrets. Why couldn't she just move on? She was only making herself miserable.

She'd made the right decision. Things had turned out well for Gage and she was glad for him. Part of her wished she'd waited at the courthouse after her deposition to say goodbye to him, but hadn't she done that already? Seeing him again would only make her pain worse. It was better for both of them that she'd left when she had. There was no need to drag things out.

She slipped off her black velvet-trimmed jacket and heels. She planned to change into jeans then go home and determine what needed to be done before she could move back in. Until her house was ready, Robin had offered her a place to stay.

"Meredith?" her friend called out. "I'm going out for a few minutes."

"All right." Tugging her black silk blouse out of her skirt, her mind whirled with thoughts of Gage. She wondered if he'd spoken yet to Aaron Chapman. His friend would be ecstatic to learn Gage was alive and returning to the fire department.

"Meredith?"

At the sound of Gage's deep voice, she whipped around, her heart beating painfully in her throat. His blue eyes flared hotly as he looked her up and down.

Swallowing hard, she committed to memory how good he looked in his dark suit with a blindingly white shirt and muted paisley tie. "How did you know where to find me?"

"Robin told me."

She frowned.

"I know. Surprised me, too." He rubbed his nape and she noticed he was sweating.

Concerned now, she took a step toward him. "Has something happened?"

"Nothing bad. The trial has been delayed until tomorrow, because of James."

The uncertainty on his face had tension winding Meredith's nerves.

He cleared his throat. "I wanted to leave the court-house with you."

"I thought it was better to go on." This was too much. She couldn't bring herself to look at him. "You saved a lot of people today."

"*We* did. We saved them. If it weren't for you, I wouldn't have been able to stop that detonation."

Meredith couldn't work up any regret over the death of Larry James, not when he'd intended to kill anyone and everyone he could.

Gage continued, "I had to take care of some things, finish giving my statement, then walk with the fire department through the courthouse until we found all the accelerant James had planted."

"What about security? Why didn't anyone notice him?"

"We think he came in yesterday before the building closed and hid in the ventilation system last night and again this morning before people arrived for work."

Gage shifted from one foot to the other. "It was hard getting away from Haynes, but I finally did."

At the mention of the fire chief, Meredith knew what was coming. Her heart fell and she had to force her gaze to meet Gage's. "I heard you were offered your old job. That's great. I really mean it. No one is better at fire investigation than you are."

"I wanted to talk to you about that."

How could this still hurt so much? She turned away. "I should finish changing clothes and get home to see what needs to be done."

She felt him walk up behind her, stiffened when he curved his hands over her shoulders. "Gage."

He hoped with everything in him Meredith would listen to what he had to say and change her mind about them. She *had* to change her mind, although he was prepared to dig in for however long it took to convince her he was totally committed this time.

"I'm crazy in love with you," he said huskily.

She stepped away and turned, the anguish in her blue eyes tearing at him. "There has to be more."

"Compromise on both sides." He wanted to go after her, pull her to him, but he didn't. "I know."

"We've tried it. It didn't work."

"You tried. I didn't. But I will this time."

Her voice quavered. "The only way we can be together is if one of us is miserable."

"No, it's not." He knew she truly believed that and he was determined to convince her differently. Only sheer will kept him from gathering her close.

"After the last year, I know what I can't live without, and that's you." Chest tight, he refused to give in to the dread pounding through him. "I have an idea."

She shook her head, looking confused.

"I'm going to open a private fire-investigation company. That means I can choose my clients and more important, my hours. We can accommodate your work schedule when we need to."

"But you were offered your old job. Did you turn it down?"

She was still listening. That was good. Despite the vicious knot in his gut, he gave her a half grin. "If you'd waited at the courthouse, I would've told you I'd made this decision before Haynes even talked to me about my old position."

"You can't leave your job."

Instead of the pleasure he'd hoped to see in her eyes, she looked horrified. "Meredith, this is a chance to start over. It's something I want to do."

"You couldn't live with that! You shouldn't have to. Quitting my job is something you would never ask me to do."

"You didn't ask, baby. I thought of the idea as I was talking to Gramps earlier."

"You should be with someone who doesn't need you to change."

"I want us to work, no matter what it takes."

"Not this. Your job is who you are. You're incredible at it."

"And I like it, but I *love* you." He took her hand, encouraged when she didn't pull away.

She shook her head. "You'd be unhappy. Our lives just don't mesh, Gage."

"They could, if you'd let them." He tamped down his exasperation. "I know what it's like to be without you. That's a price I'm never paying again."

Tears filled her eyes and he felt a burst of panic when she said, "I don't want you to do this."

"Well, I am. Can't you meet me halfway?"

"You'll resent it one day."

"Damn, you're stubborn. What I'll resent is not getting another chance. My time away has been one regret after another. If I let you walk away, that will be the biggest one of all."

She stared at him. He'd refused his old job. For them.

"You still love me. You know you do."

There was no denying it.

He dragged a hand down his face. "Is it that you really haven't forgiven me?"

"No, it's not that."

"I'm on my knees here, Meredith. Giving you whatever you want."

She *wanted* to believe things would be different this time, but she was afraid to. "Do you mean it?"

"Yes," he said firmly, his gaze intent on hers. "Just a chance. That's all I'm asking."

The wall she'd built against him weakened. "It isn't fair for me not to trust you the same way you trust me."

"We'll get there. I'll earn it."

"No!"

"Baby—"

She put her hand on his arm, the first contact she'd

initiated. Hope flared. "No. You don't have to *earn* my trust. If I decide to try again, I *will* trust you."

His heart kicked hard. "If? Are you saying… Will you give it a shot?"

"Yes."

Her voice was so soft he had to lean forward. Even then, he was afraid he'd heard only what he wanted. "Meredith?"

"Yes." She moved into him, flattened her hands on his chest. "I want to try again."

Emotion tightened his chest as he covered her mouth with his. After a long moment, he lifted his head. "I love you."

"I love you, too. I never stopped."

How damn lucky was he? "You're never going to doubt me again. I'll make it work this time."

"*We'll* make it work."

"You're really saying yes?"

She nodded, her arms going around his neck as she pulled him down for another kiss.

He turned her, walking her backward toward the bed before he realized he didn't have everything he wanted. Lifting his head, he said hoarsely, "Wait."

"Why?" She nuzzled his neck.

Holding her to him with one arm, he pulled a slim leather notebook from his suit jacket with his other.

"What is that?"

"My calendar."

She laughed, her eyes full of the light he'd almost given up ever seeing again. "What are you doing? Writing this stuff down?"

He was going for it. All of it. His lips feathered across her forehead. "I'm talking marriage, too."

She started.

He pressed her. "Meredith, tell me you mean marriage, too."

"We don't have to hurry—"

"Tell me."

His voice was husky with emotion and his face held a raw vulnerability she'd never seen before. Was his hand shaking? He was putting himself on the line, hoping she'd say yes, but probably expecting her to say "maybe" or "no."

Here it was—the total commitment she'd once wanted from him. How could she give him any less?

"I want forever." His eyes blazed down at her. "I want you to want that, too."

"I do." When she'd been so angry last year, she'd tried and failed to imagine herself growing old with someone else. She didn't want anyone else. "Yes, I'll marry you."

"What about April 21?"

"What about it?" She pushed his dark jacket off his shoulders, loosened his tie and began unbuttoning his shirt.

He laughed. "For our wedding."

She snapped to attention, her blue eyes searching his. "You want to set a date?"

"Yes."

"That's less than two months away."

He kissed her. "Yes."

"We don't have to hurry."

He tossed the calendar to the floor and wrapped both arms around her. "Did you agree to marry me or not?"

She nodded.

"I don't want to give you a chance to change your mind, but if you're not sure—"

"I just thought it might be a good idea to take some time."

"And make sure I mean to do what I say?"

She studied him and whatever she saw in his face had a soft smile curving her lips. "Okay, April 21."

"You believe me, right? Us first."

"Hmm." Giving him a look from under her lashes, she slid her arms around his neck and breathed in his ear, "Why don't you convince me? Right now."

And he did.

* * * * *

Fan favorite Leslie Kelly is bringing her readers
a fantasy so scandalous,
we're calling it FORBIDDEN!

Look for
PLAY WITH ME
Available February 2010 from Harlequin® Blaze™.

"AREN'T YOU GOING TO SAY 'Fly me' or at least 'Welcome aboard'?"

Amanda Bauer didn't. The softly muttered word that actually came out of her mouth was a lot less welcoming. And had fewer letters. Four, to be exact.

The man shook his head and tsked. "Not exactly the friendly skies. Haven't caught the spirit yet this morning?"

"Make one more airline-slogan crack and you'll be walking to Chicago," she said.

He nodded once, then pushed his sunglasses onto the top of his tousled hair. The move revealed blue eyes that matched the sky above. And yeah. They were twinkling. Damn it.

"Understood. Just, uh, promise me you'll say 'Coffee, tea or me' at least once, okay? Please?"

Amanda tried to glare, but that twinkle sucked the annoyance right out of her. She could only draw in a slow breath as he climbed into the plane. As she watched her passenger disappear into the small jet, she had to wonder about the trip she was about to take.

Coffee and tea they had, and he was welcome to them.

But her? Well, she'd never even considered making a move on a customer before. Talk about unprofessional.

And yet…

Something inside her suddenly wanted to take a chance, to be a little outrageous.

How long since she had done indecent things—or decent ones, for that matter—with a sexy man? Not since before they'd thrown all their energies into expanding Clear-Blue Air, at the very least. She hadn't had time for a lunch date, much less the kind of lust-fest she'd enjoyed in her younger years. The kind that lasted for entire weekends and involved not leaving a bed except to grab the kind of sensuous food that could be smeared onto—and eaten off—someone else's hot, naked, sweat-tinged body.

She closed her eyes, her hand clenching tight on the railing. Her heart fluttered in her chest and she tried to make herself move. But she couldn't—not climbing up, but not backing away, either. Not physically, and not in her head.

Was she really considering this? God, she hadn't even looked at the stranger's left hand to make sure he was available. She had no idea if he was actually attracted to her or just an irrepressible flirt. Yet something inside was telling her to take a shot with this man.

It was crazy. Something she'd never considered. Yet right now, at this moment, she was definitely considering it. If he was available…could she do it? Seduce a stranger. Have an anonymous fling, like something out of a blue movie on late-night cable?

She didn't know. All she knew was that the flight to

Chicago was a short one so she had to decide quickly. And as she put her foot on the bottom step and began to climb up, Amanda suddenly had to wonder if she was about to embark on the ride of her life.

From glass slippers to silk sheets

Once upon a time there was a humble housekeeper.
Proud but poor, she went to work for a charming and
ruthless rich man!

She thought her place was below stairs—
but her gorgeous boss had other ideas.

Her place was in the bedroom, between his
luxurious silk sheets.

Stripped of her threadbare uniform, buxom and blushing
in his bed, she'll discover that a woman's work has never
been so much fun!

Look out for:

POWERFUL ITALIAN, PENNILESS HOUSEKEEPER
by India Grey
#2886

Available January 2010

New Year, New Man!

*For the perfect New Year's punch,
blend the following:*

- *One woman determined to find her inner vixen*
- *A notorious—and notoriously hot!—playboy*
- *A provocative New Year's Eve bash*
- *An impulsive kiss that leads to a night of explosive passion!*

When the clock hits midnight Claire Daniels
kisses the guy standing closest to her, but
the kiss doesn't end after the bells stop ringing....

Look for

Moonstruck

by *USA TODAY* bestselling author

JULIE KENNER

Available January

---

red-hot reads

www.eHarlequin.com

HB79518

HARLEQUIN® HISTORICAL:
Where love is timeless

From chivalrous knights to roguish rakes, look for the variety Harlequin® Historical has to offer every month.

REQUEST YOUR FREE BOOKS!

2 FREE NOVELS
PLUS
2 FREE GIFTS!

♥ Silhouette®

ROMANTIC
SUSPENSE

Sparked by Danger, Fueled by Passion.

YES! Please send me 2 FREE Silhouette® Romantic Suspense novels and my 2 FREE gifts (gifts are worth about $10). After receiving them, if I don't wish to receive any more books, I can return the shipping statement marked "cancel." If I don't cancel, I will receive 4 brand-new novels every month and be billed just $4.24 per book in the U.S. or $4.99 per book in Canada. That's a saving of 15% off the cover price! It's quite a bargain! Shipping and handling is just 50¢ per book in the U.S. and 75¢ per book in Canada.* I understand that accepting the 2 free books and gifts places me under no obligation to buy anything. I can always return a shipment and cancel at any time. Even if I never buy another book from Silhouette, the two free books and gifts are mine to keep forever.

240 SDN E39A 340 SDN E39M

Name	(PLEASE PRINT)	
Address		Apt. #
City	State/Prov.	Zip/Postal Code

Signature (if under 18, a parent or guardian must sign)

Mail to the **Silhouette Reader Service:**

IN U.S.A.: P.O. Box 1867, Buffalo, NY 14240-1867
IN CANADA: P.O. Box 609, Fort Erie, Ontario L2A 5X3

Not valid for current subscribers to Silhouette Romantic Suspense books.

Want to try two free books from another line?
Call 1-800-873-8635 or visit www.morefreebooks.com.

* Terms and prices subject to change without notice. Prices do not include applicable taxes. N.Y. residents add applicable sales tax. Canadian residents will be charged applicable provincial taxes and GST. Offer not valid in Quebec. This offer is limited to one order per household. All orders subject to approval. Credit or debit balances in a customer's account(s) may be offset by any other outstanding balance owed by or to the customer. Please allow 4 to 6 weeks for delivery. Offer available while quantities last.

Your Privacy: Silhouette is committed to protecting your privacy. Our Privacy Policy is available online at www.eHarlequin.com or upon request from the Reader Service. From time to time we make our lists of customers available to reputable third parties who may have a product or service of interest to you. If you would prefer we not share your name and address, please check here. ☐

Help us get it right—We strive for accurate, respectful and relevant communications. To clarify or modify your communication preferences, visit us at www.ReaderService.com/consumerschoice.

SRS10

HARLEQUIN® Romance®

ESCAPE AROUND the WORLD

*Dream destinations,
whirlwind weddings!*

The Daredevil Tycoon

by

BARBARA MCMAHON

A hot-air balloon race with Amalia Catalon's
sexy daredevil boss, Rafael Sandoval, is only the
beginning of her exciting Spanish adventure....

*Available in January 2010
wherever books are sold.*